They waved goo  the back door. It wa porting in broad daylight wouldn't be wise.

As they walked through the eerie Scottish Mists, the silence wrapped around them like a smothering blanket. A stand of druid stones emerged from the thick fog towering above them. Chinoah shivered against him. Magic rolled off the stones in warning.

With the image of the 1878 blacksmith shop in his head and whispering spirits in his mind, their adventure began. His hands tightly wrapped around Chinoah, their duffels secured on their backs. He closed his eyes and focused his vision on Wylder, Wyoming Territory of 1878 inside Dugan's Blacksmith shop. This was his first mistake. He was unsure of the blacksmith shop's interior, as he'd never seen it.

Instead, they were unceremoniously dumped, what he hoped was only several yards outside the shop, in the worst blizzard he'd ever seen. He tightened his grip on Chinoah. *Guess I paid too much attention to the description of the building itself and let that disrupt my landing location.* The wind-driven snow swirled around them, making visibility difficult if not impossible.

# Praise for Tena Stetler

*Hidden Gypsy Magic* – "From the moment I stepped into the pages of Hidden Gypsy Magic, I fell into a beautiful, magical world. When the story was finished, I wanted to touch my kindle and disappear into the world Tena Stetler created."

~ *Mary Morgan, Author*

*A Witch's Quandary* – "Off the chart chemistry and interesting characters endowed with magical powers and distinctive voices launch from the page to cast a spell on readers' imaginations."

~*InD'tale Magazine*

*Chocolate Raspberry Magic* – "With magic, animal interactions, a stunning seaside setting, and the best cabin ever, this book had everything a paranormal romance reader loves."

~*Marilyn Barr, Author*

"Tena Stetler is a gifted writer, and her stories keep getting better and better."

~ *N.N. Light Book Heaven*

# An Angel's Wylder Assignment

by

Tena Stetler

*Wylder West Series*

**An Angel's Wylder Assignment**

Contact Information: info@thewildrosepress.com

Cover Art by *Kristian Norris*

The Wild Rose Press, Inc.
PO Box 708
Adams Basin, NY 14410-0708
Visit us at www.thewildrosepress.com

Publishing History
First Edition, 2022
Trade Paperback ISBN 978-1-5092-4005-0
Digital ISBN 978-1-5092-4006-7

*Wylder West Series*
Published in the United States of America

## Dedication

To my husband my own personal hero for his support and patience when brainstorming each story.

To the staff and authors of The Wild Rose Press for their unwavering support and assistance.

To my readers who I write the stories for so they may be whisked away into a fantasy world they may never want to leave. Thank you for your never ending support! Love you all!

Chapter One

Unexpected Visitors with an Unprecedented Assignment

Inside the family castle in Scotland, Killian put aside his warrior angel duties and relaxed in front of a roaring fire with Chinoah, a Native American wolf shifter.

He idly swirled wine in a cut crystal glass, watching the flames glint off the burgundy liquid. It was his duty to take care of the property while his cousin, Tavish, and his family were on holiday before the highland's harsh winter weather set in.

This year he'd be staying through the holidays, though Chinoah didn't know it yet.

Who says a battle-ready warrior angel couldn't handle both duty and family? *Bollocks to that.* His best friend, Caden, did it. Well, kinda. Legion Commander Nathanial North balanced both just fine.

He slipped an arm around Chinoah. She cuddled into him as he pulled the patchwork quilt Jalen, Tavish's wife, had made and given them to celebrate their hard-won relationship status of dating. One step at a time, Chinoah had requested.

The brass door knocker echoed through the castle announcing visitors.

With a raised brow, he peered at Chinoah. "Expecting guests, are we?"

"Not as far as I know." She got to her feet and padded across the stone floor.

"Wait." Grumbling, he pushed up from the cozy warm couch, slipped his socked feet back into his boots, and clomped toward her. "Best let me answer the door since we don't know who's waiting on the other side."

She slowed her pace to allow him to catch up with her. "This castle is huge. By the time we get to the door, the visitors may be gone." She giggled.

"Way to keep in shape." Chuckling, he kissed her. "Apparently, my cousin made the original great hall into their family living space."

"God help us if we're in the bed-chamber when someone comes calling." She snickered. "We'd have to sprint down the balcony hallway, across the split staircase, and through the great hall. By then, the visitors would have decided no one was home."

"Which could have been Tavish's plan." He smiled at the thought. "Besides, I didn't hear you complain last evening when you thundered through the castle for a couple of hours on four paws."

"That was different. My wolf needed the exercise, and you didn't want me to go outside." Her lips formed a pout that he found irresistible.

"Didn't want to spring you from a trap." He turned his attention out the window where the snow swirled in the howling wind. "Besides, who in bloody hell would be calling at this time of night and in this weather?"

She raised an eyebrow and shrugged. "Only one group of individuals I know."

"Oh, no. I'm on leave. They didn't know where I was going. Besides, they wouldn't expect me to be here." The ancient wooden door *groaned* then made a *squeeing* sound when Killian yanked it open. "What in tarnation are you doing here?"

Chinoah stood on tiptoe and stepped to the side to see who was at the door. "Angels always know. At least that's what you tell me," she whispered against his ear.

He shot her a warning glance and turned his attention to the situation at hand.

"Nice to see you too." Legion Commander Nathanial North stood on the stoop with Sean, two of his warrior angels, and Caden, who was now a liaison to the legion rather than a warrior, due to injuries.

At first, Killian held tight to the door. "So am I to assume this is not a social visit?" Large wet snowflakes swirled around the visitors and into the doorway.

"If you let us in, I'll tell you the reason for our visit." Nat glanced up at the snow drifting over his warriors.

"Oh, of course." He grudgingly stepped back, gently moving Chinoah over, and allowed the warriors to enter. "Can I get you something? Coffee?"

"I've cinnamon rolls frozen. Only take a few minutes to thaw and warm them up?" Chinoah offered, turning toward the kitchen.

"We'd appreciate your offerings. It's damn cold out there." Nat extended his hand.

He hesitantly took his offered hand. "Don't make me sorry I let you guys in. I'm on holiday for part of November and the entire month of December. Planning on spending the holidays with my cousin and his family."

Nat frowned and pursed his lips. "You may have to adjust your plans."

"Aww shit. I knew it. The problem is that my cousin won't be back for three weeks. I promised to take care of the castle while he's gone. It's an arrangement we have every year. Lowers my stress and keeps me from ending up like Caden." He couldn't help adding the little jab. Caden was a liaison to the legion due to what boiled down to PTSD angel style during a dark demon battle.

"This year I was planning on spending the holidays with Tavish's family." Killian reluctantly motioned the group of men to have a seat in the room facing the huge stone fireplace. "Can't it wait until after the holidays?"

"I'm afraid not. Caden and Mystic have offered to take your place here at your cousin's home. Your assignment can't wait." Nat grimaced.

He huffed out a breath. "How bad is it?"

"Bad. A high-ranking demon has used the Scottish mists to travel back in time. We suspect he will attempt to disrupt or change the ongoing negotiations in Wyoming Territory. The window of time is around 1868 to 1879, involving the Eastern Shoshone and later the Northern Arapaho. There are mineral and water rights, boundaries, and numerous other delicate issues involving the Shoshone Reservation. The other consideration is the railroad track west.

"So why me? I don't have a connection to Wyoming." He paused for a moment. "Unless you are including Chinoah."

"Sort of. An ancestor of yours actually invented the bicycle in a blacksmith forge. The trade you would be plying in Wylder, Wyoming in the year 1878. From there, we hope you can locate the demon and intervene, sending him back to the present to stand trial for his offenses."

"What offenses? Sounds like you're jumping the gun. Now we are chasing demons because we think they are up to no good? News flash, they're always up to no good." He crossed his arms and rocked back on his heels. "If we…"

Commander North held up his hand. "Enough. The assignment is yours whether you like it or not. The possibility that the demon is planning to change the past to benefit in the future is enough." The commander shrugged. "If you succeed, you've secured the right to your relationship in the eyes of the Tribunal."

His eyes narrowed. "Blackmail."

Without comment, the commander continued. "Chinoah would be a diversion because she is a Native American, you are Scottish, and she would be your wife."

"Now, wait a minute. Chinoah and I haven't even considered the subject of marriage. The Angel Tribunal forbids it. Remember?" He narrowed his eyes.

Nat grinned wickedly. "You're the one that defied the Tribunal's orders and became involved with a mortal."

"Oh, now wait just one damn minute. That was Caden. Not me. Well, it was sorta me after Caden was allowed to marry his mortal. Well, again, not exactly mortal, she is a shapeshifter as is Chinoah. What about you?"

"Tread lightly, lest you find yourself sanctioned for insubordination." Commander North paused staring down at him. "The tribunal has approved this assignment, which includes Chinoah accompanying you to the past. Be aware this is a difficult assignment on many levels. It may require several time slips for you to locate the demon. We have no clue where in time the demon has surfaced. There were so many pivotal events in that time period that shaped current Wyoming.

"It's a good guess he/she will try to disrupt history for its benefit. Chinoah will have to cover for you when you're gone. We're in the process of setting up a life for you two in Wylder, Wyoming. You'll be the town blacksmith, bladesmith, and farrier. Trades familiar to you. There is a young man in Wylder who will help you. Luke Wells is your apprentice. He is mortal but doesn't know your secrets and should smooth your arrival into Wylder as the new owner of Dugan's Blacksmith."

He scrubbed a hand over his face. "To be honest, it's been a long while since I've used any blacksmith or bladesmith talents. Those are strenuous professions."

"Better brush up your skills. Chinoah will be your bookkeeper in a time most women were not well educated, let alone a woman of her heritage. She may not be accepted in town. Nor your marriage."

"So this 'marriage' is undercover only in Wylder. Right? You don't expect us to marry just to appease the powers that are sending us on this assignment."

"That's right." Nat rubbed at the back of his neck.

Sean and the other two warrior angels snickered. Caden gave them a scathing glance.

"I can't speak for her." Killian peered across the room to the kitchen, where she was rattling pans and dishes. "Chinoah, you might want to listen to this conversation."

She swung out through the tall door, balancing a tray with steaming mugs and a plate full of cinnamon rolls. "I'm coming." Pausing at the coffee table, she set the plate down and surrounded it with the mugs. "Did you need something else?"

"You might want to sit down." He moved from his place at the fireplace, put an arm around her, and they both eased down on one end of the sofa.

"Okay, I'm sitting. What's going on?" Wide-eyed, she shifted her gaze from him to Nathanial.

Nat reiterated the info he'd given to Killian. "We need you to accompany Killian on this mission because you are familiar with the Wind River Reservation and its history. Your accounting skills are invaluable. As well as your people skills will come in handy. I won't kid you. Your heritage may not be welcome in 1878 Wylder, Wyoming Territory. It won't be easy, and you'll be on your own while Killian searches the timelines for the demon."

"Wow. You want me to go with Killian back in time? Pretend to be his wife? You do know we haven't even discussed marriage."

"We are aware. In this matter, time is of the essence. As we speak, an angel is arranging the purchase of a blacksmith shop for Killian and a cabin on the outside of town. Basically, the people of Wylder will be expecting you. The only thing they don't know is when."

"What can we take with us?" She worried her bottom lip with her tongue. "Oh, and I don't wear dresses, especially in a blacksmith shop."

"Only what would be acceptable in 1878. That will go for your clothing." Nat glanced around. "I'm not the right person to answer this. You'll need to do research. If possible, make contact with our angel, Becket, if he makes it back before you leave."

"We can research it on our own. As far as clothes, I don't see a problem with Chinoah wearing jeans at the blacksmith shop. In the town, she'll need to dress as the other women do to blend in." Killian took her hands in his and held her gaze. "You don't have to do this. But it could be quite an adventure for us."

"Can I think about it? Never time traveled. How is that done?"

"Unfortunately, as I said, this project is time-sensitive. Killian will need to leave within two days. If you're to accompany him, you'll need to be ready then too. I don't want to pressure you, but your skillset is really needed in this situation. In addition to Killian's." Nat paused at Killian's scathing look. "Sorry." Nat shrugged, palms up. "No time to sugar coat it."

"I'll need to take time off from the River Winds Casino if this mission will last into the new year. Sounds like you have no idea how long we could be gone. Any chance I could talk with Mystic before we leave? Will she be read into this situation since she and Caden will be taking over Killian's and my castle duties?"

Nat took a bite of his roll, wiped his fingers in a napkin, and scratched his head. "I don't see why you couldn't have a conversation with Mystic. She will be aware." He took a swig of his coffee and peered at her expectantly. "Are you taking the assignment?"

"Do you want me to return to Wyoming and get Mystic?" Caden interrupted, shifting his gaze from Chinoah to Nat. "She needs a bit of warning as well to take leave from her job at the Bureau of Indian Affairs. These women are not under your command. They have lives of their own and would be doing the legion a huge service taking this on. Thought I should put that out there."

"I'm well aware of what I am, or rather the Angel Tribunal is asking." Commander North glared at Caden. "You are more a pain in my ass as the legion liaison than you ever were as a warrior angel."

"Gee, thanks, sir." Caden smirked. "So what'll it be?"

"Depends on Chinoah's decision." Nat shifted from foot to foot, then stared at Killian.

Killian shrugged one shoulder and raised his hands. "It's her decision."

Chinoah blew out a breath. "Sure is a lot of hand raising and shoulder shrugging going on. Yes, I'll accompany Killian. But I have a few conditions."

Nat rolled his eyes heavenward. "Of course, you do. Let's hear them."

Chinoah held up one finger. "First, I have to explain my absence to the River Winds Casino."

"Mystic can help with that." Caden nodded.

"I love my job and have no intention of losing it due to this mission." Chinoah held up another finger. "Second, I get to have a conversation with Mystic by tomorrow morning. Third, I would like three days to research and obtain the clothing that is acceptable to 1878. Oh and today doesn't count."

Nat scowled then opened his mouth as if to object.

Caden interrupted. "Sounds fair. I'll go get Mystic." With a pop, he disappeared.

Chinoah smiled like a Cheshire cat and took a bite of her cinnamon roll, then pushed up from her seat. "Going to get my computer and start researching."

Nat cleared his throat. "We can arrange for the clothes and shoes you'll need to wear. They'll be in the closet of your cabin upon your arrival. I'll see what we can do about jeans of that era."

She tilted her head up at the commander. "What if I don't like them?"

Commander huffed out a breath and shoved up from

the chair. "Killian, control your woman."

Chinoah pointed her thumb and forefinger as if in the shape of a gun. "Got ya." A wicked grin spread across her face before she flounced across the great expanse of room and stopped at the third stairstep. "I'll get my computer and be right back." As she climbed the stairs, her footsteps on the stone steps echoed around the room.

Killian tried to hide the laughter by feigning a cough, but in the end, laughter won out despite his commander's thunderous expression. "Sorry, there is no controlling her. She's her own woman. Need I remind you she is not under your command? I assure you, she'll do her job."

"She'd better," the commander grumbled. "There's a lot weighing on this mission."

"Understood." Killian peered up the steps where Chinoah had disappeared.

"We're back." Caden and Mystic faded into the room.

"What have you done?" Holding a duffel and computer bag, Mystic glared at Nat. "Where Chinoah?" She dropped the duffel on the floor.

"I only had time to give her a quick synopsis of what was going on. Mystic sent an e-mail to her supervisor requesting time off for personal matters. Since she never takes time off, there should be no problem. If there is, at least she's in the same time and can handle it from here. Unlike Chinoah."

"Two days…That's all the time you gave them?" Mystic tapped her foot.

"Caden," Nat warned.

"Mystic, Chinoah is upstairs. Why don't you see if you can find her? Have her show you around a bit so we don't get lost in this behemoth of a castle."

"Good idea." Mystic beamed at Caden and slid a withering glance to Nat.

"She'll be in the first bed-chamber to the right at the top of the stairs," Killian offered, scrubbing his hand over his unshaven chin. *What the hell I have gotten myself into?*

Chapter Two

Surprise Assignment Settles in With Travel Arrangements, Wardrobe, and a Plan.

Standing in the middle of the bed chamber, hands on hips, Chinoah huffed out a breath, staring into her closet. "I'm going to take a pair of my jeans and one comfy shirt for returning to present day, whether they like it or not. How are you supposed to work in a blacksmith shop with a long dress on?" She stuffed them into a duffel. "Travel light, they instructed." She shoved the rest of her essentials into the duffel, when someone tapped her on the shoulder. She squealed, dropped the shoes, and fisted her hand before swinging around.

Mystic held out a hand, fending her off. "Whoa there, Chin, it's just me. What's got you on edge?"

"Can you believe it, two days to get ready to travel to 1878 and encounter God knows what. I'm no angel. A damn good shapeshifter. But how do I defend myself against white settlers in 1878? They aren't or weren't friendly to my kind."

Laughing, Mystic patted her friend's shoulder. "Well, in their defense, our kind gave the white ones a bad hair day, to say the least. That would make anyone a little leery."

Chinoah swiped at her. "Not my fault or my time." She blew the raven hair out of her face, shoving the

12

waist-long strands over her shoulder. "I have to set all my things in order and be ready to leave in two days. Did I tell you that?"

Mystic put her finger to her chin. "Yes. I've heard that somewhere. But think about this, you're embarking on a one-of-a-kind adventure with the love of your life. Even better, it's with the Tribunal's blessing. Do you realize what this means to mortal women and warrior angels' relationships?"

She sucked in a breath and settled down. "Do you realize how this could sabotage relationships if this goes badly?"

"It won't. You, of all people, can handle this assignment. With Killian by your side, you two will make history. Get it? Make history. I crack me up." Mystic giggled.

"You're the only one." She shot back. "Now, are you here to help or harass me?"

"Advise you. Blending in is a requirement. Your words, actions, and demeanor when dealing with the townspeople either make your assignment go smooth or rough. A chip on your shoulder because of the clothes on your back will do no one any good." Mystic eyed the duffel.

"How am I supposed to get clothes, shoes, and even acceptable underwear for 1878? She crossed her arms over her chest defiantly.

"It's my understanding that there is an angel in Wylder 1878 preparing all those items and procuring a cabin for you on the edge of town within walking distance of Dugan's Blacksmith shop." Mystic suggested calmly. "If something goes horribly wrong, I've got your back. Nat and Caden both have promised to send me to you if necessary. But you've got this."

"The blacksmith business is supposed to be ready for us to just slip into," she conceded. "With me in the wild west and you in Scotland taking care of this behemoth. Who's handling the accounting and overseeing the Wind River Casino?"

"Sage. She has everything under control at the Casino. The Bureau of Indian Affairs is sending a liaison to check in weekly for as long as I'm needed here. So make quick work of this demon and get back here."

"Killian looked forward to spending the holidays with his cousin and family. Now that's out the window."

"It was your choice to get mixed up with a warrior angel and all it entails. Too late to back out now." Mystic winked at her best friend. "As if. "She snorted. "What an adventure you're about to embark on. I can't wait to hear all about it. Maybe Caden and I could stay for the holidays too. Regardless of how long it takes, I believe you can time it to arrive back in the present when you want."

She brightened considerably. "Really? We could celebrate the holidays in 1878 then return here and celebrate them again?"

"Theoretically. I've no first-hand knowledge of time travel, only hearsay. You understand? You'll know for sure soon." Mystic snickered. "You better get a wiggle on, girl. The guys will want us downstairs for briefing soon."

"I've packed a few must-have items. Guess the rest will be up to whomever is on the other end of 1878." She huffed out a breath. "A man picking out women's underwear. No thank you. I'll take my own. Who will know?"

Mystic pawed through the duffel. "This is it? Don't you have a couple of long patchwork skirts with a few cute embroidered long sleeve blouses you wore at the casino for pioneer days? I also remember a full-length coat, a pink gingham dress with a matching sun bonnet, and a white apron. At least those would be made with decent breathable fabric."

Inside the closet, she took out the specified articles of clothing. "It's going to be fall, maybe even winter weather, in Wyoming, that's not sun bonnet weather." She grumbled, wrenching her favorite parka out of the closet.

"You can't take that coat. I'm sure your wardrobe in Wylder will be satisfactory for the weather there. Come on. I hear footsteps on the stairs. We don't want Nat to get his tighty-whities in a knot." Both women giggled.

She plopped on the bed, and a big tear rolled down her cheek. "I'm scared. This whole experience is so far out of my wheelhouse. What if I screw up and get us killed? Um, me, killed?"

"Killian would never let that happen," Mystic assured her.

"But Killian will be off who knows where hunting down the demon, and I'll be in Wylder circa 1878 holding down the fort. I'm not sure I can do this. Maybe you should go?"

"With Killian? No way. He's your warrior. I have enough trouble with Caden, and he's only a consultant to the legion now. You've got the necessary skills to do this. Killian would kill me after he got a look at the books when I was through."

She smiled through her tears. "You got that right. Okay. I got this. If I don't, you got my back?" She shoved

Tena Stetler

off the bed, folded the extra clothes, and added them to the duffel. "I'm ready on that score."

Killian strode through the doorway.

"Hey, don't you knock?" Chinoah and Mystic chimed.

He took a few steps back, held his hands up in a gesture of surrender, and glanced at the door with a puzzled expression before meeting their gaze. "It was ajar, so figured you weren't holding secret meetings. Nat wants to go over the broad view of the assignment with us tonight. Tomorrow we'll get into the possible reasons the demon used the Scottish Mists to time travel to his current location.

"Then a crash course in life in 1878. The problems you may encounter as a Native American educated woman. What Wylder has to offer as far as shops, hardware, the railroad situation, and townspeople's opinions, which before you ask, do matter."

"Everyone will be staying the night?"

"Possible. Caden and Mystic will be staying. In the morning, we can show them around, acquaint them with the property, and duties in the daylight. Can't vouch for Sean or Nat."

"An almost-midnight snack is in order." She tossed her duffel at Killian and motioned Mystic to the doorway. "Might as well get a handle on the kitchen." Bounding down the wide stone stairs, she skidded to a halt on the landing, her shoes squeaking in protest. She paused to wave at the angels, then sprinted to the enormous kitchen with Mystic in hot pursuit.

Killian brought up the rear and shrugged his shoulder. "She's not ready to come to terms with the mission yet. But she will. Why don't we all convene in

16

the kitchen? The women are fixing a snack. We can talk there. I'll build a fire in the hearth, and it'll be cozy warm as in here." He paused a moment. "Are you staying the night? The only reason I ask is we should start the fires in the rooms you'll occupy to supplement the heating system. Stone walls and floors suck up the heat for a bit."

"After a bite, setting out your assignment, and what we know, I'll be heading back to Alaia and Kat. Tomorrow will be soon enough to go over the rest." Nat pulled up a chair to the long, polished wood table eyeing the platter of meat, cheese, bread, and condiments Chinoah slid across the table.

She pointed Mystic to the cupboard where the mugs and glasses were stored. After turning on the coffee maker, grinding the beans, and adding them to the filter, she pushed the button to brew. A few minutes later, the room filled with the aroma of freshly brewed coffee and the sounds of a crackling fire adding warmth to the room.

Chinoah stacked the plates next to the platter then spread the silverware and napkins at the end of the table. "Grab it and growl." She chuckled. "There's hot water in the silver cylinder, tea bags in the basket, and hot chocolate in the pump insulated pitcher." Pouring herself a mug of hot chocolate, she slapped together a sandwich and eased down in a chair to observe the angels and their commander.

*How the hell did I get myself into this mess?* She mulled it over for a moment or two, then decided. *I'd not change a thing. Though after this escapade, who the hell knows.* Sandwich in hand, she took a bite and realized just how hungry she was.

Nat inhaled his food and drink, filled another mug with coffee, and took a sip. Waiting for the table to be cleared, he took a map out of his briefcase, spread it out on the table, then tossed a copy of the demon's dossier to Sean, Caden, and Killian. Cautiously, he handed one to Chinoah. "So you'll know what we're dealing with. I doubt you'll come in contact with him or her, but…stranger things have happened."

Killian shot a warning glance at Nat. "She'll be out of range. I'll see to it."

Nat shrugged his shoulders. "Currently, the consensus is that the demon is headed to 1868 to disrupt the negotiations for Wind River Reservation land. At that time, they were unaware of the rich oil and gas reserves on the property. In 1878 the Northern Arapaho were relocated to the reservation, welcomed by Chief Washakie of the Eastern Shoshone. This was a move filled with trepidation though history claims differently. Don't see a benefit of meddling there.

"However, there is a point to be made he is after something to do with the railroad which runs right through Wylder, Wyoming." He raised his arms and let them fall. "Then again, it could be anything in between. The one thing we do know, nothing good can come of his time slipping through history. A high-powered demon won't act and risk his standing without a huge reward of some kind."

"If Killian will be timing it all over the 1800s, why do you need me?"

"Fair question. You need to make him look settled, a businessman with a purpose, below the radar of any magical kind. Also, stir the pot as a Native American wife of a Scottish businessman. That alone will raise all kinds of eyebrows. Once you're settled in, accepted, and known as a woman with an education, I believe the other women will eventually accept and confide in you. Or at least befriend you out of curiosity. Whichever the case, eyes will be on you, not on Killian, and he'll be free to move about as required."

"And what about the blacksmithing duties? Bookkeeping I can handle, but blacksmithing, not even if I had the ability." She crossed her arms over the chest defiantly.

Nat let out a good-natured laugh. "We wouldn't think of putting you in that position. There is a young man, Luke Wells, who is or was an apprentice to the old man that previously owned the blacksmith shop and recently retired. He'll handle the job while Killian is away on business. But you will be the boss. A position that will take time to earn his respect with the help of Killian."

"What a tangle of a disaster just waiting to happen you are dropping me into."

"I, as well as the Tribunal, have it on good authority you can handle it." Nat gave her a beguiling smile.

"Not going to work on me. You're throwing us into the lion's den with the hope we make it out alive." She shook her head. "I have one stipulation."

"You are not in the position to set any stipulations," Nat stated flatly. He turned his attention to Killian with a raised brow.

She fisted her hands on her hips and stared him down. "Oh really. I beg to differ. The stipulation is that if Killian and I make it back to our own time before the holidays, you will leave us alone to spend the holidays with Killian's family. If not—it's a moot point."

Killian turned away, attempting to hide a smile, she surmised. Mystic gave her a two thumbs up signal, then busied herself with the dishes.

"Sleep on it." Chinoah flounced across the room and paused at the door. "Killian, I believe we need more wood to boost the fire in the main room and stoke the fires in the rooms for our guests."

"I assume you will be on your way." Killian glanced at his legion commander.

Nathanial gave a curt nod.

"Our uninvited guests can help stoke their own fires. Caden and Mystic, I'll show you where the woodpile is outside and the log storage upstairs for each room." He turned his attention to Nat. "See you in the morning." Killian turned on his heel and strode toward the door, wrapping his arm around her waist, propelling her out the door. "You do realize, I'm going to pay for your little demonstration and act of insubordination. In front of his warriors, I might add." He smirked.

"Then he shouldn't expect me to go along on this difficult assignment without a question. Doesn't work that way in the mortal world. Being married to Alaia, a mortal, and having a child with her, I'd assume he's aware."

"Still, he expects his warriors to obey his every order and assignment without question. Which can be life or death in battle." He paused and turned her toward him.

She bristled. "As previously stated, I'm not one of his warriors. Am I?" Standing on tiptoe, she brushed her lips over his.

"Nope, you sure aren't." Taking gloves out of his back pocket, he scooped up an armload of wood then jerked his chin at the other angels. "Might want to use gloves." Sean, Jon, and Riker followed his example.

Caden glanced around at the vast expanse of land before grabbing logs.

"Lead the way," Caden said cheerfully.

After guiding the angels to their sleeping chambers, Killian stopped at Caden's bedroom door as the women joined them and bustled inside. "Tomorrow morning we'll give you a quick tour. Not much to do but keep trespassers at bay and enjoy the peace and quiet. Tavish is aware I've been called away and that you will be taking care of the place until I return. No reason to cut his holiday short."

"You'll be heading into the mists tomorrow early evening after conferring with Nat?" After depositing the wood in the bin, Caden took his gloves off and glanced at his friend.

"Probably the sooner, the better, with Chinoah and Nat at odds. It appears we won't know much until we get there and do a little investigation." Killian shrugged one shoulder.

"Strange assignment." Caden agreed. "At least we know when you will be, mostly."

"Yeah, Chinoah will be at the time and location, even if I have to time slip farther back or ahead to locate the demon." A jaw-popping yawn caught him by surprise. "Chinoah, you ready to call it a night? We got a long, adventuresome day ahead of us tomorrow."

"You'd be right about that." She hugged Mystic and Caden. "See you for a bit in the morning."

"Thanks for covering for us. We owe you." Killian clasped Caden's shoulder.

"Speak for yourself. I got drafted into this assignment too. Maybe we can time it to get back here to celebrate the holidays together." She closed the door behind them and turned to Killian. "What if we get lost in time? Is that possible?"

"I'm an angel with great navigational skills. Not to mention a few hidden talents. We'll be fine."

Chapter Three

At Odds With the Assignment, the Truth Comes Out

The next morning the sun's bright orange, yellow, and pink rays spread across a rare clear, cerulean sky as Chinoah blinked her eyes open and glanced out the window. Dread and uncertainty from last night were gone, replaced with a sense of adventure and excitement. She turned her head and stared at the Scottish Highlander in her bed, all brawn, sculptured facial features enhancing his large, expressive, bright blue eyes now hidden by sleep.

He stirred, reached out with a muscular arm sprinkled with a light dusting of reddish hair, and encircled her around the waist. Pulling her tight against him, he grunted and nuzzled her neck, never opening those wicked blue eyes. Only a smile curved his full lips. She kissed him, and his eyes slid open.

"Morn darl'n. Feel better about our assignment?"

"I do, yes. Not sure why. Guess I needed to sleep on it." She moistened her lips with the tip of her tongue. "Guess we better get the day started. Your commander will be here soon, and we've so much to show Caden and Mystic before we leave. We forgot to tell them about the chickens, collecting eggs, and sheep in the pasture. "All need the animals to be fed." She snapped her fingers. "They need to know the food is in the barn."

"There's time enough." He said in a deep, lazy Scottish brogue. The water pipes clanged in the old castle. "Tavish was going to get those pipes checked and fixed if they needed it before we have a major flood in here. Winter isn't the time for a pipe emergency."

"Look on the bright side. We could have an ice skating rink in the great hall for the holidays." She snickered.

"True, but no water for a month would overshadow the icy fun. Maybe Caden can arrange to have them checked." He leaned up on one elbow as a booming voice came from the first floor great hall. "Shit. Nat is here. Best get this over with so we can be on our way."

"But...Are we leaving soon? Thought it would be tonight when prying eyes wouldn't be a danger." She picked at a corner of the bright patchwork quilt, then shifted her gaze to him.

"The mists will cover us. Won't be anyone in them less they're supposed to be there." He beamed at her, patting her hand, and tugging her close to him. "We'll have a grand adventure."

She pried herself from his firm grip, pushed the heavy comforter aside, and swung her legs over the side of the bed. "Everyone will want breakfast soon anyway." Toeing her slippers on, she picked up her fluffy robe and marched into the bathroom. At the doorway, she turned to peer at him. "Wanna join me?" When she turned back to the bathroom, he stood right in front of her in all his naked glory. He was quite the sexy package. Slowly letting her gaze slide over him from head to toe, she brushed her hand over his broad chest and let her fingers slip lower.

"Never turn down a woman's invitation. Nat can

wait."

She glanced at him with trepidation. "He wouldn't just appear in here. Would he?"

"Not if he knows what's good for him." He chuckled. "He is the legion commander. Very little is hidden from him. However, we are still working our way through warrior angels' ability to marry with the Angel's Tribunal's blessing. After being forbidden for so many centuries it's a slippery slope. We must be available and battle-ready at a moment's notice, wherever we are. But with wife and eventually family, concessions have to be made on both sides."

"Understood. So he can't—won't—just appear in our shower?" She repeated.

This time he roared with laughter. "Unequivocally no. He wouldn't have the audacity to do such a thing even to the single warriors, or the respect he demands would go right out the window. Bad for morale with individuals that have your back in life and death situations."

She blew out a breath. "Good to know." Stepping out of the water's spray, she twisted the shower handle. Icy cold water splashed on the tile floor. She giggled. "Glad we moved, or you'd be in no condition to participate in what I have planned." Leaning into him, she raised on tiptoe and caressed his chest and shoulders as her hands slipped around his neck. He raised an eyebrow and slipped his hands under her arse, lifting her off the floor, encouraging her to wrap her long legs around his waist.

****

After stepping out of the shower, he toweled off and walked into the bedroom to yank on jeans, pull a blue cable knit sweater Chinoah had made for him over his head, and plopped on the bed to put on socks and shoes. "I'm not going to keep the commander waiting any longer. So I'll meet you downstairs. He's going to want to brief us both at the same time, then get on with his day. Pretty sure we aren't the only business he's tending to today."

"I'll be right behind you." Steam billowed out of the bathroom as she strolled into the bedroom, toweling her hair, water still dripping off of her naked body when she passed slowly by him.

He reached out and grabbed her, tugging her to him. "Tease. You're so naughty." After kissing her neck, he shoved her toward the closet. "Get dressed before I make us really late." He clucked his tongue at her before swatting her on the behind. "Hurry."

Once outside the bedroom door, the alluring aroma of freshly brewed coffee wafted up from the family area, then he heard voices below. Sean, Jon, and Riker were already up, and someone had made coffee. Probably Mystic. He double timed it down the stairs and skidded into the great hall where the warriors and Caden were seated in front of a roaring fire conversing about upcoming missions.

"Good morn everyone. Sleep well?"

"Like a log." The warriors said in unison, then laughed.

Killian raised an eyebrow. "You rehearsed that?"

"No, we have better things to do with our time. Except right now, we are babysitting one of our own and his main squeeze to make sure they don't get cold feet." Sean snickered at Killian's thunderous expression.

Holding up a hand palm up, Sean said. "Only

kidding." He shifted his gaze to Nathanial North, whose expression mirrored Killian's. "Sorry, sir."

"What's this about a main squeeze?" Chinoah breezed into the room. Her long hair French braided at the sides of her head flowed into a thick braid down her back. Black jeans fit her curves, and a lavender sweater swung around her hips. "I have a name, Chinoah Grace. But you can call me Chinoah. Clear?"

"Yes, ma'am," the warrior echoed.

The commander's lips twitched and a half-smile curved up one corner of his mouth. "Guess the young lady, ahem, Chinoah, put you in your places. Let's get down to business. We're burning daylight." He took another look at her, male appreciation showing in his eyes for a split second. "You can't wear that type of clothing where you are going."

"Let's not start that again. I'll not wear dresses in the blacksmith shop. Nor do I intend to wear my good jeans and sweaters. I've been dressing myself for quite some time without assistance. Thank you very much."

Mystic stood at the entrance of the kitchen. "Breakfast is ready. Better get in here before it gets cold." She sent a sympathetic glance in Chinoah's direction then shook her head. Waiting for the men to clear the doorway into the kitchen, Mystic caught her by the sleeve. "A word."

"Sure. I know several." Chinoah giggled.

Mystic pulled her into the other room and hissed, "You've got to quit antagonizing Nat. He's pretty good-natured, but Killian will pay for your insubordination. Your attitude doesn't do any of us any good as far as the warriors being able to wed. You've a chance to show how useful a talented mortal woman can be."

Chinoah's eyebrows shot almost to her hairline as a look of indignation screwed up her face.

"You know what I mean. We're not mortal, but shifters, but for all intents and purposes, we are. Don't blow it. The commander's not going to check your bag before you go. Take what you want. You'll be the one to catch the other women's ire in 1878. So just knock it off."

Chagrined, her shoulders slumped. "Sorry, I didn't even think of what this assignment could mean going forward. Sorry. He just rubs me the wrong way."

"You two got off on the wrong foot. Work with him. Give him a chance. You'll see." Mystic hip-checked her. "Breakfast is waiting, if the guys haven't eaten it all."

"What?" Chinoah squealed.

"Got ya. There's plenty." Mystic smugly danced across the floor, grabbed a plate, and began to fill it. Chinoah was right behind her and swatted her on the shoulder.

"That was plain mean."

"I know. Couldn't help myself." She turned and whispered. 'The devil made me do it." Mystic dissolved into a fit of giggles.

Nat raised an eyebrow then shook his head, sending a stern glance in Caden and Killian's direction.

The room was quiet except for the scraping of silverware on plates and the occasional request for more eggs or bacon. Once they were all finished, Sean, Jon, and Riker's chairs scraped on the stone floor as they headed for the living area.

"Where are you three going?" Nat addressed the warriors.

Sean cleared his throat. "Uh…to the living room to

wait for you and the others."

"Wrong. You three now have kitchen duty." Nat jerked his chin toward the kitchen. "We are guests in Killian and Chinoah's temporary home. Mystic made breakfast. I've business with Killian and Chinoah as well as Mystic and Caden." He shrugged. "Leaves you with kitchen duty."

Chinoah started to protest. "They don't know where everything—"

"They'll figure it out. Smart warriors, they are." Nat motioned Killian, Caden, Chinoah, and Mystic into the living area, where the commander had spread out maps, documents, and other necessary paperwork. For the next couple of hours, the group strategized, argued, threatened, and finally agreed on a plan going forward.

Finally, the commander stood and stretched his legs. "I believe we've got as much worked out as possible with the limited information we have. Becket, our warrior who's set everything up for you, will remain in Wylder for a few days while you get settled. Cover story is he is your cousin. Because he was stateside and you were in Scotland, Becket went ahead of you and your wife to scout out the town and viability of the blacksmith shop and living accommodations. He'll return every few weeks to see how things are going. Should this assignment go terribly wrong for any reason and we have to pull you out, Becket will be the one to assist you."

"What about us?" Mystic stood hand on hips. "If Chinoah, needs help—"

"Killian will help her. If it is necessary for you to join Chinoah, Becket will let us know. We don't want any more unfamiliar faces in town than necessary which could put the demon on alert. Killian and Chinoah need to ingratiate themselves into the town and the hearts of the townspeople in as short a time as possible."

"Having a sister visit can't be out of the normal." Mystic argued.

"It's not— It's the ability to time travel you to the exact time, place and minute, Chinoah and Killian are once they are settled and life moves on. Understand?"

"Understood, but I don't like it. How are they supposed to get back? They'll not have the mists to assist."

"Actually, they can port to the Scottish Mists and leave from there once the assignment is complete."

"What about the demon and his minions? Prisoners or terminated?" Mystic persisted.

Chinoah's eyes went wide. "Terminated?"

Nat glared at Mystic. "Women are so much more trouble than my warriors." He rubbed the back of his neck. "That decision will be up to Killian. He knows what he's doing and will act accordingly. Believe me, if we didn't need Chinoah's expertise, none of this would be happening. Now I have to go. I have no doubt Killian will handle this assignment as he has his others."

"You still haven't answered my question," Mystic pressed.

The commander's face became stony and he blew out a resigned breath. "Okay, Mrs. Silverwind, Chinoah Grace, this is how it will go. If Killian deems it necessary he will terminate the demon and any of his minions. If he foresees a battle, prior to engaging— " Commander North emphasized each of the last three words "—he will send word with Becket. That way we can arrange reinforcements, if possible."

He held up his hand before Killian could object. "I

30

am aware sometimes advance warning is not possible. But do your best to avoid a battle, because you are a security force of only one. If the demon and minions are to be prisoners, Becket and reinforcements will return the demon and his accomplices to stand trial. Doubt it will come to that. Demons will battle to the death. Now is that what you ladies wanted to hear?"

Silence reigned for several minutes. The wind howled outside as the sunny day turned into a brewing storm. Lightning danced amid the dark clouds.

Chinoah was the first to find her voice. "At least I know what to expect now. For me, the unknown is scarier than the known. Do you understand?"

"I'm doing my best. But you two must recognize, I've never in all my hundreds of years been in this kind of situation. Times are changing, and we have to adjust, to navigate the new landscape, so to speak, using whatever or whoever is at our fingertips to get the job done." He shoved his fingers through his hair and rubbed at the back of his neck.

"I don't like it any more than you two or four do. But the assignment has to be done, and you two are the best we have to succeed. The longer we stand here discussing the situation, the more time the demon has to get ahead and embedded somewhere to launch his plan." Frustration and irritation flowed through his last sentence. "Now, if there are no further questions, I'll take my leave. Sean, you stay here and assist Caden and Mystic. Also, a standby should Killian need help. John and Riker, I'll see you above in twenty minutes." With that, he raised his arm and disappeared.

"Wow." Mystic blinked. "Sounds like should be more than two of you, but I can see his point landing in

1878 with too many people."

"We'll be fine." Chinoah forced a smile. "Won't we?" She glanced at Killian.

"Yep. Been in worse situations before, like the oil field in Riverton, WY. Feels like we'll be fine." He winked at Caden. "Come on. We'll show you what you need to know until Tavish and his family return." Killian reached for Chinoah's hand, laced his fingers with hers and led the way.

Chapter Four

A Walk Through the Scottish Mists With Unexpected Results

Rather than dispute Nat with the need or permission to carry weapons, Killian had simply slid his jewel-encrusted, magic-infused sword in its scabbard and slung it across his back. Slipping his dagger into its sheath at his ankle, he also holstered his gun at his other ankle, straightened, and shrugged into his black leather duster. The wrist arrows and other warrior weapons were sewn into the coat's lining. After all, he was a warrior angel and must have his tools of the trade. He smirked.

Chinoah stood wide-eyed at his cache of weapons. "And I got scolded packing unapproved clothing. Do you have any idea what your commander would do if he—"

"Sure enough. Notice I waited until he left. You're the one that chose the jeans battle with him." He shifted one shoulder nonchalantly. "Learning curve to pick your battles." A low chuckle rose from his throat. "Besides, he'd never ask a warrior going into battle to leave the tools of his trade behind."

"A little advance warning would have been nice." She crossed her arms across her chest defiantly.

"Prep time was a luxury we didn't have when this assignment was dumped on us. Wouldn't you say? Nat had us at a disadvantage and he knew it."

As if the words just sunk in, she blanched. "We're not—you're not—really going into battle. Right?"

"No way to know until we get there. Demons are not known for their negotiation skills. The Riverton skirmish is a prime example of their single-mindedness."

"But that was a build-up of theft, deceit, and trickery by a tribe member acting as the River Winds Casino manager who was driven by power, greed, and jealousy. Ethan played into the hands of the manipulative demons. He was outmaneuvered from the beginning. In the end, he got what he deserved."

"That's how it works. Evil prays on the unsuspecting. In our case, we'll have our ducks in a row long before flushing the demon out in the open and forcing him to show us his hand. Enough of this. As Nat said, we are burning daylight."

They waved goodbye to their friends and slipped out the back door. It was a bit of a walk to the Mists, but porting in broad daylight wouldn't be wise.

As they walked through the eerie Scottish Mists, the silence wrapped around them like a smothering blanket. A stand of druid stones emerged from the thick fog towering above them. Chinoah shivered against him. Magic rolled off the stones in warning.

With the image of the 1878 blacksmith shop in his head and whispering spirits in his mind, their adventure began. His hands tightly wrapped around Chinoah, their duffels secured on their backs. He closed his eyes and focused his vision on Wylder, Wyoming Territory of 1878 inside Dugan's Blacksmith shop. This was his first mistake. He was unsure of the blacksmith shop's interior, as he'd never seen it.

Instead, they were unceremoniously dumped, what

he hoped was only several yards outside the shop, in the worst blizzard he'd ever seen. He tightened his grip on Chinoah. *Guess I paid too much attention to the description of the building itself and let that disrupt my landing location.* The wind-driven snow swirled around them, making visibility difficult if not impossible. A large dark mass faded in and out of the sheets of snow not far from them. It wasn't easy to gauge anything in all this white. To his relief, he heard or thought he heard, a voice above the roar of the winds. A dark figure appeared to be moving in their direction through the wet curtain of white.

A man bundled up in cold weather gear until you could barely see a pair of eyes came trudging through the foot-high snow with a rope tied to his waist. The other end of the cord disappeared in the driving snow. When the man reached them, he tied them all together. Hand over hand, they followed the rope back to the porch of Dugan's Blacksmith Shop.

"Where the hell did you two come from in this storm?" The man surveyed right and left, then stomping his feet on the wooden planks outside the door, extended a hand. "I'm Luke. You must be Killian and Chinoah." Luke untied them and gathered up the rope. "Let's get inside."

Killian nodded.

Luke turned the handle and shoved hard at the door. It flew open and crashed against the wall. The wind blew the white flakes inside, covering the entrance floor. He turned and paused. Warmth enveloped them. "I didn't figure you'd make it here 'till the storm was over. You must be half-frozen."

"You got that right." Quickly, Killian hefted their

35

duffels and followed Luke through the door, his hand at Chinoah's back, guiding her ahead of him.

"Built a roaring fire this morning. Good thing I live in the rooms above the shop since the blizzard hit mid-morning. I was kinda watching for you. A man would have to be crazy to venture out in this stuff." Red crept up Luke's neck and spread across his face. "I mean….storms like…"

"Understood. We had no idea when we started out… Just happy we made it here, and you rescued us. Our bodies wouldn't have been found until spring thaw."

Luke struggled to close the door against the howling wind. Killian dropped the bags, braced a shoulder against the heavy wooden door, and helped Luke push. With a *bang,* the door closed. Luke dropped a metal bar across it.

Killian raised an eyebrow shifting his gaze from the horizontal bar to Luke.

The man grunted out a laugh. "The wind whips hard in these parts. Sometimes the latch won't hold it shut. The stout bar and brackets on either side of the door make sure it stays closed." He tugged off his gloves, yanked off his hat, and shook out his brown hair. Chunks of snow melted on the floor, forming puddles. After unwinding the scarf from around his neck, Luke took off his coat, carefully placing them on an iron rack a few feet from the welcome fire.

*Hopefully, I won't have to explain why we are only chilled, not frozen from the storm.* Killian gave thanks to God for the outerwear given to them by the Daughters of the Pioneers Association. He helped Chinoah out of her wet coat and directed her toward the hearth.

Luke's gaze swept over her and his mouth dropped

open at what Killian could only guess was her attire of men's pants and hand-knitted sweater. The man averted his gaze to the floor, rubbing his hands together in front of the fire.

"My wife only travels in clothes that won't leave her vulnerable. She also dresses in pants in the shop, so her dresses don't get destroyed. Heaven knows I spent enough on her clothing to learn the hard way. Do you have a problem with that?"

"Ah… No sir. Not used to seeing a woman dressed like a man. That's all." Shifting from foot to foot, the young man peered at Killian. "If I may, a word of advice. Since you're not from around these parts. Don't let her go to town in those clothes. Some of the townswomen have a mean streak and will—I mean she is—an Indian—it's going to be tough enough without her wearing strange clothing."

"Understood. We'll heed your advice. Tonight, where can we bed down? I'm beat, and sure my wife is exhausted."

Luke ran his fingers through his wet hair. "Your cabin is a few blocks away. But until the storm blows over, you and your wife can take the rooms upstairs. I'll bunk down in the back room."

"We don't want to put you out of your home. We can…" Chinoah paused at Killian's subtle shake of his head and pressed her lips together.

"Thank you, I appreciate it. If you'll show us to the rooms. The rest of the business can wait until tomorrow.

"I guess. Your cousin wanted to be notified the minute you arrived. Believe he'll just have to wait. Though, he'll be plum worried if he's heard about the storm."

"I'll contact Becket as soon as possible. You wouldn't have something to eat around here, would you?" Killian asked as he followed Luke up the stairs and motioned him into open loft-type living quarters.

In front of the bed, resting on a rug, was a furry dog. When they entered the room, it lifted its head and stared at them with sad eyes, then lowered its head on its front paws.

Seemingly oblivious to the dog, Luke's unsure expression turned to chagrin. "Of course. You and your wife get settled. I'll warm up the stew and cornbread one of the neighbors brought over early this morning when word spread there would be a new owner for the shop. People will be glad you've come to town. I was just the apprentice to the former owner. Not a very good blacksmith, yet." Luke turned to go back downstairs.

"We'll rectify that in short order." Killian clapped the young man on the shoulder.

"Wait. Luke, what about the dog?"

"Oh, that dog has hung around here for a couple years. The former owner started letting it in on cold winter days. I couldn't leave it out in this storm. So I brought the pup inside. I guess this is where it wound up." He moved his foot alongside the dog. "Come on downstairs. I'll find you something to eat." The dog raised its sad eyes to the group, moaned, and closed its eyes.

"I think the dog misses the previous blacksmith." Chinoah knelt down and carefully caressed the dog's head and behind its ears. "Don't you? What's its name?"

"Don't know. All I ever heard him called was dog. No way to take the dog with him, so left it here."

"Awww, that's so sad—downright mean. All

creatures have feelings, and this one is hurting." Chinoah plopped down next to the dog. "We'll make sure this never happens to you again."

Killian cleared his throat. "Don't make promises you can't keep. We don't know what the future will bring." He raised an eyebrow.

"I won't abandon this poor creature. Pup's known way too much hardship in her short life." She paused, slapped a hand over her mouth, and peeked at Killian, then switched to Luke. "At least it seems that way."

The dog raised its head, licked Chinoah's offered hand, and rested its muzzle on her lap.

Luke smiled. "Guess so. Anyway, the dog seems to like you. I'd better see to the food. Come down when you're ready." His footsteps echoed in the building as his boots clomped down the stairs.

"I could help him." Chinoah offered. "Isn't that woman's work in this time period?"

"Probably. But he offered. Knows where everything is. And you are exhausted from the trip here. Remember?" He glanced at the dog. "You understand her thoughts?"

She peered up at him. "Of course. I'm canine."

"Didn't know you had that ability. So what are you going to call her?"

"There are several things you have yet to discover about me." Chinoah's brow furrowed. After a few minutes of thought, she snapped her fingers. "Adventure. Addy for short." She turned to the dog. "Do you like that?"

The dog nudged her hand with its nose. Her fingers scratched behind the dog's ears. "First order of business is brushing and a bath. You stink." She laughed.

"How do you intend to brush and wash the dog? People in this time don't care for their pets like we do in—" He glanced around, making sure Luke was out of hearing distance. "—the time we come from. Bathing for us is different here than home."

"Too bad. I brought a couple of extra brushes, and a dab of my shampoo can't hurt. Maybe even a little conditioner, or we'll never get those tangles out."

He blew out a breath and leaned over the dog. "Best off cutting those mats out. Easier on you and the dog. But not tonight."

She put her hand to her forehead. "Oh yes, I've had a harrowing experience, and I'm tired." She covered her mouth as a fit of giggles ensued.

Leaving the matter of the dog for tomorrow, he was relieved she could find humor in the current situation. He sat on the sagging bed and took off his wet snow-covered boots. He waved his hand over the bed, and the old worn sheets shimmered into pristine sheets, pillows, and comforter.

"How are you going to explain that?" Chinoah demanded, getting to her feet.

"Not going to sleep on those sheets. Doubt Luke will ask. But if he does, we packed them with us." He glanced out the window. "No telling how long we'll be here before we can make it to our cabin. Or what blacksmith emergencies may come up in the meantime. Sounds like this town has been without a blacksmith for a while."

"Killian and Chinoah, food is ready. Come get it while it's hot," Luke called up from the kitchen.

Chinoah took Killian's hand, motioned the dog to follow, and padded down the stairs.

The aroma of beef stew and cornbread filled the

shop. On a metal table covered by cloth were three bowls, three small plates, eating utensils, and mugs. A coffee pot sat on a metal contraption of some sort close to the fire.

A kettle hung over the fire with a long-handled ladle sticking out of it. Luke stirred the stew, then ladled steaming food into the bowls and handed them to Killian and Chinoah. The young man took a cast iron pan from the hearth with gloves and placed it on the table. He uncovered the pan to reveal warmed cornbread. "Don't have a stove upstairs, so this works just fine for me. I usually eat meals at my parents' house across town or with Jilly. She's my girlfriend." His cheeks pinked.

"We look forward to meeting her." Chinoah pointed to two dented old tin pans. One filled with water, the other empty. "Are those the dog's bowls?"

Luke turned to see where she was pointing. "Yeah. I'll feed him, uh, her after we're done eating."

Chinoah picked up the empty pan and held it out. "She looks as hungry as we are."

Without hesitation, the man filled the bowl. She set it on a metal bench to cool.

Addy's eyes sparkled as she stuck her nose in the air and sniffed.

"You'll have a wait a few minutes until it's cooled. Don't want to burn your mouth." Chinoah blew on the hot food before taking a seat at the makeshift table. "Everything smells great. Thank you so much."

"Yes. Thank you." Killian eased down in a chair as soon as Luke had gotten a bowl for himself and settled down. "Tell us what to expect for business demands in the town? Repairs, crafting new items, horseshoeing, or knife forging?" He snatched a cornbread muffin from the pan, sliced it in half, and smeared butter on it. Taking a bite, he nearly moaned. "This is really good. Who'd you said made these?"

"Cissy, your neighbor down the way. She owns the bakery in town. Great cook. And generous too." Luke scooped up a spoonful of stew and popped it in his mouth. "To answer your question, the shop does a little bit of everything. Ol' Joe, that's the former blacksmith's name, wasn't good with animals, so he kept the horseshoeing to a minimum or sent me out to do it.

"Before Joe's health took a turn for the worse, we were pretty busy. Even now, I stay busy. Things will pick up once people know you are here. Other than Dugan's, the closest blacksmith is in Cheyenne. That's quite a trip for families. Townsfolk prefer to do business locally with people that they know and trust. It may take a while for them to warm up to you. But they will."

Chinoah spooned up a bite of stew. "This is delicious." She looked over at the dog, reached out and grasped the bowl, stuck her finger in it, then slid it across the floor to Addy. "There you go, girl." She walked over, pumped water and washed her hands in the sink, returned to the table, and carefully took a cornbread muffin and bit into it. "Wonderful." She added butter to the rest of the muffin.

"Dog will be spoiled in nothing flat," Luke observed.

Chuckling, Killian motioned toward the dog. "You can bet on it. Good for the pup to keep Chinoah company." A jaw-popping yawn caught him off guard. He scraped the remainder of the stew from the bowl and followed it up with the last piece of muffin. Taking a swig of his coffee, he glanced a Chinoah. "Guess it's time to turn in."

"Sounds good to me." She soaked up the last of her stew with her muffin and slipped it in her mouth. After getting to her feet, she picked up the mug and finished off its contents, looking dubiously in the sink. "Do you wash dishes in—there?"

Killian choked on his last swig of coffee and stood. Black streaks covered the sink. Carelessly tossed to the side of the sink was a piece of what looked like chain mail. A bar of well-used soap rested in a metal dish.

"Oh, not usually. Don't eat down here. I take it upstairs after heating it." Luke glanced in the sink. "It's just stained, not dirty. Your cousin, Becket, and I cleaned this place from top to bottom, anticipating your arrival. Never had a woman work inside the forge." He shrugged. "Didn't know what to expect." The young man pointed to newly erected walls with a door and window in the building's far corner. "We made you an office away from the possibility of flying embers and forge heat."

Chinoah hurried over to the area and opened the door. Inside, a small wooden desk, complete with ledgers, paper, and pencils, was arranged in the room's center. What appeared to be a couple of filing cabinets lined the back wall. A brand new upholstered chair rested behind the desk with two wooden chairs in front. "It's wonderful. I didn't expect—I mean—I could have made do with what was already here."

"Ol' Joe wasn't much for accounting. He kept most of it in his head until recently, and he hired me to help out. The ledgers are in the bottom drawer in the filing cabinet on the right. Figured you'd want to start your own set of books." He snapped his fingers. "Nearly forgot. A Shoshone shaman from Healing Waters, part of the Shoshone Reservation, sent a telegram. He'd like to meet with you when convenient. The Reservation, it ain't the safest, and Healing Waters is several days ride away from here, just so you know."

"I'll get in touch as soon as this storm subsides." Killian walked to the window and peered out. "Not going to be soon. The snow is really coming down." He put his arm around Chinoah, guiding her to the stairs. "Goodnight. Sorry about commandeering your sleeping quarters."

"Offered, not commandeered, sir." Luke smiled. "Nite Mrs. Dugan.

"Killian, not sir." He shot back.

"Chinoah, not Mrs. Dugan." She waggled a finger at Luke. Addy pushed her way in front of them on the stairs and bolted into the rooms above the forge. In the bedroom, Addy had already staked her claim to the multi-color braided rug in front of the bed.

"Guess you won't be using that to avoid the cold floor in the morning." He laughed softly and gathered Chinoah in his arms. "Well, Mrs. Dugan, what do you think?"

"If you think you're going to take advantage of the situation, think again. We're not married." She huffed out a laugh relaxing against him, then glanced around. "No bathroom up here?"

"Nope. Remember, the amenities you're used to are limited here. Indoor plumbing and hot running water are relatively new. Only for the rich. Except, Becket made a few upgrades for us in the forge and probably at the cabin. Didn't expect us to arrive in the blinding snow."

"I sure hope so." She yawned, leaned down to stroke

Addy, then raised and brushed her lips over Killian's. "I'm for bed."

"Me too. Tomorrow will be soon enough to take in our surroundings." He snorted.

Chapter Five

A Snowy Beginning to Life in Wylder

It was pitch dark when Chinoah woke. Her breath
hitched in her throat as panic took hold. Where was she?
She jerked up. Killian snored softly beside her, lessening
her panic. Memories of the last twenty-four hours came
flooding back. Shoving her hair out of her face, she
crawled out of bed, wrapped her robe around her, then
remembered there wasn't a bathroom up here. She nearly
yelped when her bare feet touched the cold floor.
Something soft, furry, and warm nuzzled her feet. The
dog. She sent comforting thoughts to make up for the
sheer panic she'd felt and probably relayed to the dog
earlier.

Abruptly, Killian sat up. "What's wrong?"

"Gotta pee."

"Oh, I'll escort you downstairs." He stretched,
grabbing his robe from the bottom of the bed.

"Inconvenient," she muttered.

"Hopefully, we won't be here long. Since we don't
know our way around, trudging through the few feet of
snow in subzero temperatures doesn't seem prudent."

She laughed. Her breath puffed out in a white cloud.
"Heat?"

"Woodburning stove over in the corner." He paused
to toss a few logs on top of glowing embers in the stove.

Flames slowly appeared at the edges of the wood. After making sure the fire started, he closed the cast iron door. "Should have heat soon."

As she walked down the stairs, the ambient air grew warmer. Gravitating toward the warmth, she nearly missed the bathroom. Killian's hand shot out and directed her in the right direction with a quiet chuckle.

After exiting the bathroom, Killian followed her over to the cast iron stove that was emitting warmth. "Luke knew to bank the fire before he went to bed. Smart." The angel took a couple of logs from a pile and shoved them inside the stove. Flames flared up around the wood. "It'll be warm down here when he gets up, and we get to work."

She wandered over to the window. At least three feet of snow had fallen, and it was still coming down, but not as heavy as last night. Her eyes became accustomed to the dark, and she could see the partial outlines of buildings across the street. *At least I don't feel as isolated as last night.* There was no clock on the wall, so she had no idea what time it was. By the thin line of orange spreading across the horizon, it must be close to dawn.

Killian came up behind her and wrapped his arms around her. "Warmer over by the stove." He nuzzled her neck, trailing kisses up to her cheek.

"Not appropriate for me dressed like this to be seen by a single male, better head back to our rooms." She shivered.

"Good idea. Hopefully, the stove has warmed the room a bit." He swept her up in his arms and carried her up the stairs two at a time. Once at the top, he pushed open the door to find the dog curled up next to the stove, where warmth radiated into the room. Lowering her feet to the floor, he left her standing behind the heat source. With an iron hook, he pulled open the door to the stove, shoved more wood inside, and closed it, rubbing his hands together.

The weak sun's rays streaked through the window, spreading across the bed, and warming the room a bit more. Her stomach growled. "What are we going to do for breakfast?"

"Luke seems pretty resourceful. Bet he's got eggs and bacon stashed around here somewhere."

"I hope so. Don't think the stores will open today." She grimaced, ripping the comforter off the bed, and wrapping herself in it. She settled next to the dog by the stove.

He frowned for a beat then chuckled. "Oh, so that's how it's going to be. Every dog and woman for themselves. Leaving the man out in the cold."

"Believe the man—uh—angel can fend for himself." She giggled but opened up the comforter to him and a place by the warmth of the stove.

As they sat together warmed by the fire, the aroma of eggs, bacon, and freshly brewed coffee wafted into the rooms.

"Guess Luke is up. Do you suppose some of what he's cooking is for us?" Chinoah, inhaled deeply. "Mmmm…Better get dressed. Don't want the food to get cold." Taking another deep breath, she threw the comforter off and raced to her duffel. "Guess he'll have to put up with a woman dressed in man's clothing." She dumped the bag on the bed and chose blue jeans, a long sleeved underwear shirt, and a bulky pink sweater. "Guess its layers today. It's so cold the windows are frosted up on the inside."

He raised a hand and blew gently on the window. The frost cleared. When he continued to peer out the window, he made up his mind. This time he waved his arm and blew at the same time toward the outside. The howling wind stacked the snow against the buildings, creating snowdrifts over ten feet high in places. Yet now, the road was reasonably clear.

Turning back to Chinoah, he smiled. "He'll live. Bet more acceptable attire for you is at the cabin. Probably should try to get there soon." He picked up the comforter and tossed it back on the bed before searching his duffel for clothes. After donning jeans, a long-sleeved waffle weave shirt, he plucked out a heavy sweatshirt.

She did a double-take out the window. "You did that. Didn't you? Is that allowed? Angel magic for your benefit?"

His mouth fell open. His eyes widened under a furrowed brow as he feigned shock. Hand to his heart, he sucked in a breath. "I'd never. Well, maybe, but in this case, not for my benefit. For the townspeople's. They need to get their stores open. From what Luke said, this storm hit early. Will have caught people unprepared." He pointed to himself. "It's a welcome gesture to our new town." His head popped out of the sweatshirt, and he pulled it over his chest.

Eyeing him dubiously, she glanced out the window again. "Funny the snow isn't sticking to the roads now."

"Any heat we get from the sun peeking out will keep it that way."

"Killian, Chinoah, I have breakfast ready if you want to come down," Luke called up the stairs.

Wasting no time, Addy thundered down the stairs, followed by Chinoah, and he brought up the rear. Once on the bottom floor, he glanced around in appreciation. Luke had a cast-iron skillet of eggs on top of the wood-burning stove, another on the metal table filled with sizzling bacon. A basket of leftover corn muffins sat in the middle of the table.

"Wow, you don't need to cook for us. But we appreciate it." Chinoah smiled.

"I gotta eat, so might as well fix enough for all of us. Looks like we'll be holed up in here for a while. Snow's piled pretty high." Luke shook his head. "Ain't seen a storm like this in my whole life, and I grew up here."

"Yes, but in places, you can see the ground from the wind drifting the white stuff. In the heat of the day, maybe we can get out and see what's what." Killian jerked his chin toward the window.

Luke raised an eyebrow and strode over to the window covered in ice. He scraped the ice off and gave out a low whistle. "Looks like the wind did us a favor. You might be right. The roads appear to be clear enough to travel, but we'll have to help the business owners dig out from the snowdrifts." He paused then rushed to another window.

"Probably should see to feeding any horses in the livery. I made sure none were outside when the storm hit. In fact, that's what I was doing when I saw you two. Don't see any life over at the stables. Buck must have made it home. He co-owns the livery. His wife is Cissy, and they own the Wylder Side Bakery." Luke lowered his voice. "Buck used to be a famous gunslinger."

"Really." Killian raised a brow. "And now?"

"He was tired of that kind of life. It's why he came to Wylder in the first place." Luke shrugged. "He met Cissy. The rest is history."

"After breakfast, I'll help you check on the horses if Buck isn't there. Chinoah can keep the stoves stocked, so it stays warm in here. Looks brutal out there."

"Thanks." Luke eyed Killian's attire. "I hope you have warmer coats than you had on yesterday."

Killian took a seat in the same chair as last night beside Chinoah. "I hope so too. My cousin was supposed to arrange for the cold weather gear. Didn't want to lug all that from Scotland. Obviously, not the wisest decision I've ever made." He patted Chinoah's knee and grinned.

Luke took the skillet of eggs off the stovetop and waved a spatula toward the wood-burning stove. "Storms blow in and out of here so often. I always keep the icebox stocked."

After breakfast, Chinoah took the dishes to the sink and washed them while the men trudged over to the livery and stables to ensure all was well. After finishing, she pulled on a parka, hat, gloves, and boots, the ones Killian insisted she needed, and walked outside with Addy trotting beside her.

Standing on the porch, she wondered where their cabin was and what the possibility of getting there on foot would be. The thought was kiboshed almost immediately. Her breath nearly froze in a white puff in the air, eyes watered, and her nose stung. A few snowflakes still falling glittered in the deceptive sun. The wind tugged at her coat.

Addy turned around and thundered back inside. "Well, that answers that," she said to the empty building as she closed the door but didn't drop the bar down, hoping the door would stay closed until the men got back. She took off her coat, hat, and gloves and hung them on the metal rods next to the fire.

She watched out the window as bundled up business owners began to make their way to the buildings with snow shovels, brooms, and other tools. Killian and Luke joined the little knot of individuals and went from building to building, unblocking the doors and windows when possible. She turned from the windows to stoke the stove in the forge. Then she went upstairs and shoved as many logs as would fit in that stove. *What have I gotten myself into? Wyoming winters are brutal in the present with the right snow removal equipment and modern creature comforts like furnaces. Here...* She glanced around the room. A sudden feeling of foreboding washed over her. A shiver shot up her spine.

The door banged open. Several footsteps echoed in the forge. "Come on Addy. We need to see who's here." The dog reluctantly got up from her place next to the stove, stretched, and followed her down the stairs. Six men were grouped around the stove discussing the recent storm and whether to open their stores.

As she entered the room, all eyes gravitated to her. Killian swiftly moved to her side and clasped her hand. She squealed and tugged her hand free. "You're frozen."

"It's brutal out there, as you know." He turned his attention to the other men. "This is my wife, Chinoah." Pausing for a moment, he watched their faces go from mild interest to disdain in a few. "She's also my bookkeeper. I see her traveling attire surprises you. Gotta tell you, after replacing ruined dresses numerous times from her walking through the forge, pants and sweaters are much more cost-effective." He laughed. "We sent most of our stuff on ahead with my cousin, Becket. Suppose it's all at the cabin."

The other men nodded and murmured their

understanding. One man continued to stare at her.

"She's a redskin. We don't abide those in our…'"

"You'll not refer to my wife with any derogatory words, or…" Killian drew himself up to his full six feet six, towering over most of the men.

The man appeared to pull into himself, his shoulders hunched. "Sorry." He turned on his heel and strode out of the forge, banging the door behind him.

One of the other men cleared his throat. "Billy's family was killed by… Indians when he was just a boy. No love lost there. Best your wife stays clear of him."

Killian wrapped his arm around her. "We've encountered a few problems that way. But once they get to know Chinoah, they usually warm up."

The men looked at each other then switched their gaze to him. "You'll find most accepting of her heritage, but married to a Scotsman…Well, you understand."

Gaze scalpel-sharp, he shrugged. "No, I don't."

The door banged open again. "Thanks for checking on the livery. Didn't think we'd be getting out until the wind came up and made the street passable. I'm Buck Standish, co-owner. And you are?"

"Killian Dugan and my wife, Chinoah." He offered his hand, and the man took it.

"Your cousin said you were on your way. Didn't expect you to show up in the blizzard." Buck sidled over to the stove.

"Me either. Didn't know it was coming. Train dropped us off, then decided to weather the storm here. Tracks froze up. Luke rescued us."

"Luke's a good kid. Smart as a whip. Caught on to blacksmithing easily, according to Ol' Joe. Gonna keep him on. Right?"

"Of course. Saved my ass, he ain't going nowhere."

"Right fine cook too," Chinoah said with an easy laugh. "Nice to meet all of you. Wish I could offer you something to eat, but all we have ready is coffee. Even that's thanks to Luke. Storm kind of caught us off our stride."

"Didn't expect it would be this bad." One of the other men piped up.

*Well, this is going better than it started out.* "If you'll excuse me, I'll go get mugs of coffee to warm you up." She switched her gaze from the group of men to Luke. "You want to show me where you keep the mugs and coffee so I can make another pot?"

"Sure." He walked to the far corner of the forge and pointed at a tall, wide cabinet. "Make-shift kitchen in there. Icebox to the right."

"Thanks. I can take it from here." *I hope.* She opened the cabinet.

When Luke returned to the group, one of the men clapped him on the shoulder. "Gonna make Jilly a right fine husband one day." The others in the group laughed as Luke's face turned bright red.

She had to purse her lips and turn away to keep from laughing. *This place was going to take some getting used to.*

Chapter Six

Much Sunnier Start to Life in Wylder

Chinoah sat in the office reviewing files and unpaid invoices.

The constant double hammering lessened from the forge, and footsteps echoed through the building. Killian appeared in the doorway, leaned one muscular shoulder against the frame, and gazed at her. "You make a mighty pretty picture sitting there." He paused a moment then sauntered into the office.

"Why, thank you, sir." She grinned. "Sounds like you are picking up the lingo around here."

"Well, some is bound to rub off." He massaged his shoulder. "This is hard work. How about we take a walk over to the bakery and get a snack?"

"I packed lunch for all of us from the meats, cheeses, and bread that Luke has stored." She pointed out the door where the lunch basket sat on top of the icebox. "Don't think it's…"

"Sweet tooth is acting up." He shrugged. "Besides, I need a break. Gonna take a while to get used to this type of work. I've a lot of respect for my ancestors that spent their entire lives as blacksmiths." Rounding the desk, he nuzzled her neck, breathing a lingering kiss just below her ear lobe.

"Soft, are you?" She chuckled.

"Not where it matters." Lifting his face from her neck, he sent her a seductive smile. "Just give me a chance. I'll show you."

In a quiet indignant whisper, she said, "Killian Dugan, must I remind you that we are only pretending, not official. According to what you told me and Nat emphasized, a commitment to physically consummating a relationship with an ang—your type of individual holds an eternity of strings. I'm not ready. Are you?"

"Didn't hear you complain when I used the loophole of pleasure," he grumbled under his breath. "Getting there. That's why we were in Scotland spending the holidays with family."

Choosing to ignore his loophole comment, she shot back. "Not there anymore. But this will be a real test of our relationship."

The other hammer ceased its racket, and she stood glancing around him. More footsteps sounded toward the office.

Luke stuck his head in the office. "Wondered where you went."

"Chinoah and I were just considering a walk to the bakery for snacks. Interested?"

"Hell yeah. Want me to go?"

"No, Chinoah wants to stretch her legs, and I want to look around town while the sun is shining. Maybe locate our cabin and let you have your rooms back."

"That wind will cut right through you," Luke warned.

"To hear you and the men around here talk, that's a common occurrence. So guess we better get used to it." He helped Chinoah on with her coat as the door to the forge banged open.

"Hey, Killian you in here?"

Luke turned in the doorway and grinned.

Killian strode to where his apprentice stood. "Well, if it isn't my cousin who should have been here to greet us."

"If you'd timed your arrival until the storm cleared, I'd been here." Becket shot back. "Didn't figure you'd brave the blizzard."

"Didn't know about the blizzard. Luke here saved us from freezing to death. No help from you." Killian glared at Becket.

"Divine intervention missed one. Sorry." He snickered.

"Bad snow storms out here are no laughing matter. Don't know where you're from, but here, mother nature demands respect and gets it." Luke said sharply.

"Didn't mean to make light of it. Just a family joke."

Luke appeared appeased and Becket continued. "Now that I'm here, why don't we take a walk to your cabin. See if there is anything else you need before I return to my other obligations. Or have you already been there?" He looked expectantly at Luke.

"I wasn't about to send them out in the aftermath of the blizzard on vague directions you scribbled down last time you were here."

"You were busy. I waited a couple of hours, and it appeared you had your hands full." Becket shuffled from one foot to the other. "Did that woman ever calm down? She was screaming about some farm equipment that was supposed to be done months ago?"

"Yeah, we got it taken care of. Ol' Joe left a few jobs incomplete and failed to tell me about it." Luke turned to Killian. "We may still have a few unfinished projects Joe didn't remember. Especially when the spring thaw comes, and farmers or ranchers are ready for their equipment."

"Wonderful. Not going to make us popular with the locals." He shook his head.

Becket stepped forward and looked Chinoah up and down. "So this is the expert Nat saddled you with? Not a complete hardship."

Killian sent Becket a warning glance. "Not sure what you're talking about. You know my wife, Chinoah. She's my bookkeeper."

"Ohh—y—yes." Becket stammered. "Got so many irons in the fire, I get confused. I had to drop everything. Close the business deal. Find you a place to live since I was in the states and you were traveling from Scotland."

"Sorry about that. Couldn't be helped. Gotta strike when the iron is hot, you know." He put a hand on Becket's shoulder and turned him toward the door. "Speaking of the cabin, let's take a look. We're anxious to let Luke have his rooms above the forge back."

"Oh shit...I mean, wow, sorry, didn't realize. The blizzard was inconvenient for a lot of folks. Speaking of the townspeople, have you met Buck and Cissy? That woman can bake. And Buck is a stand-up guy. Cissy should help with Chinoah's integration into life in Wylder. Some of the other women..." He waffled his hand back and forth.

Killian shoved Becket out the door then turned to Luke. "Can you keep an eye on things for a while? We'll be back later. Did you want something from the bakery?" He paused to put on his coat, gloves, and hat, then laced his fingers through Chinoah's gloved ones and tugged her along.

"Lunch prepared in the basket on top of the icebox." She reminded Luke. "I'll bring back one of Cissy's chocolate cakes to enjoy. Fair enough?"

"Sure. Thanks. I'll finish the project I'm working on, then take a break. But I'll stick around in case we have customers. Okay, boss?"

"Works for me. We'll get our stuff out of your way when we get back." He closed the door behind them. "What in the hell are you doing, Becket? Trying to sabotage the mission before it gets started?"

Becket took a couple of steps back. "No. I didn't realize that Luke wasn't in on the assignment. Being a go-between is a tough assignment too. One I didn't— Never mind. It won't happen again." He shivered, glancing around. Then hat and gloves appeared out of thin air.

Killian frowned. "Don't do that again. You didn't let anything slip to the other townspeople while you set all this up, did you?" he growled.

"No, of course not. I was able to purchase the land and cabin, so there's no landlord problem if you outfit the cabin in a few luxuries." He waggled his eyebrows. "I made sure you have indoor plumbing, running water, and hot water in the cabin."

"Thank you." *Figure Nat made those arrangements, but why is Becket taking credit for it? Not sure Becket has our best interests. I'd feel better if Caden had my back.* He shrugged. "Shall we check out the cabin you procured for us?"

Bundled up against the wind, Killian, Chinoah, and Becket started for the cabin. Walking up the road to Wylder Street, Becket motioned left at the end of a dirt path where a large cabin stood alone.

"I would have thought there'd be a group of cabins this close to town." Chinoah glanced around at the prairie surrounding their home. "Are you sure this is it?"

"Yep. See the pink and blue ribbons tied to the door handle? Becket pointed to two bedraggled strips of cloth. "Comes with ten acres."

Killian raised one eyebrow. "You have the key to the lock?"

"Of course." Becket drew a key out of his pocket and opened the door. Closing it, he shivered and waved a hand over to the wood stove. A roaring fire ignited. "That's better. The wood cubby is full of wood. I've made sure there is food in the cupboards and meat, milk, cheese other staples in the large icebox. Furnishings are what well-to-do people in this time would own. So hope you have a good back story. You might want to consider creating the illusion of an icebox over a real refrigerator. This place is primitive." He shook his head. "Glad it's you and not me."

"Thanks. I'll stick with the icebox." He glanced around at the wooden kitchen table, and matching chairs completing the kitchen area. Woven throw rugs, a massive oak desk took up part of a wall in the living room, upholstered sofa and chairs faced two wood-burning stoves—one at each end of the room between them a massive fireplace.

"Fireplaces leaks cold air like a mother." Becket whistled. "Imagine that's why there are two wood stoves in here."

When Killian stuck his head into the bedroom, he found the large bed had an intricately carved head and footboard, with a mattress and patchwork quilt like the one Chinoah made. The matching dresser was beautifully carved wood with several drawers. A wood stove also filled one corner of the room. A closet had been built into the wall resembling modern day. "I guess our family is considered well-to-do."

"Which, if you don't mind me saying, will make townspeople wonder why you took a Native American wife. Seems it will create more trouble if you ask me. There's a second bedroom furnished similarly and a third smaller one with only a bed. Clothes, toiletries, that kind of thing acceptable to this time period are hung in the closet or stored in the bathroom in the larger bedroom you'll be sharing with your wife."

He paused as his gaze slid slowly down Chinoah's womanly shape. Becket shook his head. "Should you decide on other sleeping arrangements, you must keep the illusion of sharing the marital bed." He snickered. "Friends with benefits. Right? Remember, you're newlyweds and expected to act as such. Nat's words, not mine."

"Didn't ask your opinion. Are we finished here?" Killian's brow creased as he narrowed his eyes at Becket.

"Yes." Becket paused and snapped his fingers. "No. There is an old-time compatible safe that has currency for this assignment." The angel handed Killian a slip of paper. "Combination. So you don't depend only on Dugan's Blacksmith for funds. Not sure how long this assignment will take, but you should be all set. I will check in with you from time to time. I'm your only contact to present day."

Returning to the living area, Killian took a piece of paper, pencil from the desk drawer, scribbled a note, then passed his hand over it. The writing disappeared. He folded it and handed it to Becket. "Please give this note to Nat. He'll be expecting it. So he'll know we arrived safe and sound if somewhat chilled."

Becket took the note, stared at it for a minute, and tucked it in his pocket. "Will do."

Chinoah sidled closer to Killian before glancing at Becket. "Thank you for your help." But the words fell in the empty room. "I don't care for that individual. He's not telling us something. Is he really an angel?"

"Appears so. Angels are individuals too. But I agree with your assessment." He held her close and kissed the top of her head, trailing kisses along her cheek and jawbone. "Alone at last. In a cozy cabin of our own."

"It's getting warmer in here too." She blew out a breath, and it no longer clouded the air. "Can we leave the fire in the stove while we're gone? I've had enough cold for today."

"I can bank the fire, make sure the door to the stove is closed, and add a little angel magic for safety. Now we better get to the bakery and back to the forge. Unless the whole town needs our services, we'll call it an early day and relax at the cabin tonight."

"Sounds perfect." She stood on tiptoe, wrapped her arms around his neck, and brushed her lips slowly over his, lingering for several beats.

He deepened the kiss before letting her go. "Chocolate cake awaits."

Hesitant to leave the cozy warming cabin, she stood behind him as he tugged the door open. Sunshine spilled across the floor into the cabin. He stuck his head outside. "The wind's died down, and the sun is warm. Walking back won't be bad at all."

She pulled her hat down over her ears and wound the brightly colored scarf around her neck, tucking it in her coat. "Shouldn't we have our own horses?"

"It's a thought. Maybe we could borrow two for the duration." He paused. "But, that sort of thing may not be done here. We'll play it by ear."

"Sounds like the way to go since we already have another furry body to return to the present with us."

"You're serious about taking the dog back with you?" He scrunched up his face.

"Yes. Addy's already seen much hardship in her young life. I see no reason to cause more. Besides, I made her a promise. She'll leave with us."

He looked around. "By the way, where is she?"

"At the shop next to the stove. She didn't want to go out in the cold again unless necessary, which it will be when we get back unless Luke let her out."

"Probably did. He is used to caring for the dog. Which brings us to another point."

"A moot point. Adventure's destiny is already forged." She giggled at her little pun.

"Not funny." He slowed the pace and glanced up. "Here we are." Pushing the door open, he startled as a bell rang over the door. A young woman bounced to the counter, her white-blonde hair swinging around her face set with sparkling blue eyes.

"Hello. Are you Cissy?" He asked his Scottish bur more pronounced than usual.

"Can I help you?" She paused for a moment, then waggled a finger. "I bet you are Chinoah and Killian from the blacksmith shop. Welcome to Wylder."

"Gee, what gave us away?" Chinoah smiled at Cissy, then gave him a sidelong glance. "We're in search of a chocolate cake. Heard you make the best in the Wyoming Territory."

"Well, that's not exactly true, but I try." She hurried to the back and returned with a two-layer chocolate cake with fudge frosting. "Will this do?" Cissy sat the cake on the counter and wiped her hand on her apron.

"Sure will. Thanks." He paid her for the cake.

"I like your Scottish accent." Cissy wrapped the cake in paper. "I could listen to you talk all day." She glanced outside. "Thank goodness the wind stopped."

The bell above the door clanged again. An older lady with graying hair pulled back in a bun at the nape of her neck, pushed through the door. "Cissy aren't you coming to help with the quilt?" The woman stopped in her tracks and stared at Chinoah. "My lord what are you wearing?" Then she switched her gaze to him. Without taking her eyes off the two she said, "Didn't mean to barge in. I'll come back later."

"No, no, we were just leaving." Chinoah put her hand through the crook in his arm.

"Oh, don't be silly. Patty Chambers, this is Chinoah and Killian Dugan. He bought the blacksmith shop from Joe."

"Nice to meet you, Mrs. Chambers." He offered his hand.

Patty took it daintily. "Where you from, young man?"

"Scotland." He watched her eyes and didn't like what he saw.

Cheerfully Cissy continued, "Chinoah works as his bookkeeper. At least that's what Buck said. Also said she dresses in men's pants and shirts so as not to mess up her pretty dresses."

"Bookkeeper, huh?" Mrs. Chambers narrowed her eyes. "Learn that on the reservation? Did you?"

"Not exactly. Does it matter?" Chinoah caught her gaze and held until the older woman looked away.

"Of course it doesn't." Cissy crossed her arms over her chest. "Anyone could do a better job at bookkeeping than Ol' Joe. Buck always had to straighten the livery's account out before Lloyd found out. Lloyd and Joe used to go rounds. I think they both liked to argue."

Chinoah laughed. "Known a few people like that. Usually, they are never wrong either."

"Yep, that is Lloyd and Joe to a T. That is until Joe's health started to fail. He could barely talk between wheezes. Left town to stay with relatives. Poor guy." Cissy untied her apron and hung it over the chair. "Guess I'd better get to Sharlet's place. Not the best quilter, but I can hold my own. Hey, would you like to join us?"

Mrs. Chambers sputtered. "No room."

Chinoah said quickly, "Not today. I've got work to finish up. We took time off to look at our cabin at the end of Wylder Street."

"Sort of behind the school at the end of the dirt road." Killian pointed in a vague direction. "Kinda tired of sleeping in Luke's rooms, and I'm sure he's tired of the cot in the forge. He was kind enough to offer when we arrived in that terrible blizzard. No way we could find our way to the cabin that night."

"Oh, your cousin, Becket, that's his name, right?"

He nodded without comment.

"Told us about the cabin. Pretty nice, I hear. A wealthy man from California had it built with all the latest gadgets. Never moved in. His gold mine went dry. He had to sell the cabin and land dirt cheap. Wish we'd known." She shrugged. "Wasn't meant to be."

Chinoah smiled smugly. "If you like to come over

sometime—"

Patty huffed and stalked to the door. "Not likely."

Cissy jutted her chin out. "I'll take you up on that one of these days. I'd love to see the cabin. Maybe get some ideas for our house." She snorted. "Buck would love that. Patty, tell the women I'll be along shortly."

Patty nodded and closed the door with a bang.

"Don't you never mind Patty. She's always fussing about something or someone. Nice to meet you two. I'm sure I'll see you around. Oh, make sure to mark your calendar for the Harvest Ball. They had to reschedule it to mid-October. That's in a couple of weeks. Great place to meet everyone in town. At a social gathering, everyone will be on their best behavior. Hopefully. Oh, and if you need a gown, Widow Lowery owns the dress shop. The girls over there would have time to put one together for you. If you tell them soon."

Chinoah strolled toward the door. "I may have to do just that. Thanks for the cake. See you soon."

Killian held the door open for Chinoah, then turned and waved. "Bye, Cissy."

"You can mark Cissy down on the friend column."

"Yep. Mrs. Chambers not so much. Not sure if I even want to try to get along with her, maybe just avoid her altogether." Chinoah sighed.

"Town's too small for that. You'll win her over." He took her arm and wound it around his waist as he slung his arm over her shoulder. "What say we eat cake and forget Mrs. Chambers."

"Sounds good. I might poke at Luke a little about her." Chinoah grinned, snuggling against him as they strolled back to the forge.

Chapter Seven

Business is Booming, and Life Sizzles in the Cabin

Killian pushed the door open at Dugan's Blacksmith and both were surprised to see a line. "Wow."

Chinoah sucked in a breath. "Guess we should leave more often."

Luke glanced up and relief flooded across his face. "Thank God."

Killian scooted behind the counter, introduced himself to those who didn't know him, and started taking orders, while Luke got the customers' completed items.

Chinoah strolled across the floor, resisting the urge to run from all the shocked looks conveyed by the few women accompanying their men to pick up items. Or maybe they were customers on their own. She didn't take time to figure that one out.

Finally, she made it to her office and closed the door. Standing with her back to the door, she relaxed and slid down the door to sit on the floor. This was harder than she thought it would be. Or maybe she was making it that way. For the first time, she hoped there were actually dresses in the cabin appropriate for work in the blacksmith shop.

Scratching sounded on the door. She opened it a crack. Adventure trotted in and looked up at her, then over to the wood stove. She closed the door quickly.

"You're right, girl it's chilly in here." Chinoah opened the stove, stirred the embers, and added wood.

A light knock sounded on the door. Her first reaction was to stand quietly and pretend she wasn't inside. Since the whole town, well, it felt like it, had seen her enter the office, that wasn't going to work. Another knock vibrated against the door. She straightened, brushing the dirt from her backside, then crossed the room and opened the door to a young woman.

"I talked with Cissy at the quilting bee. She wanted me to stop by and chat with you about a gown for the Harvest Ball and perhaps one for our Christmas Ball. I'm between projects and thought if we could talk about what you're looking for, I could start work on it, have a fitting ready in a week or so, and the gown ready in time for the ball."

*Bless Cissy.* Chinoah sucked in a breath. Her uncertainty and dread of trying to make friends in this challenging place melted away with the woman's smile.

The woman put her hands to her cheeks. "Oh, dear, I came barging in here without even introducing myself." She offered her hand. "I'm Laurel Holt. My husband Caleb is here talking about farrier services. Caleb and Joe didn't get along very well. But shoeing all our horses himself is time-consuming when he's got a ranch to run. I work as a seamstress for Mildred Lowery. She owns the dress shop in town." Laurel blew out a breath. "Anyway, I could get started right away if you're interested." She lowered her voice. "I understand you had a little run-in with Patty Chambers." Laurel waved her hand dismissively. "The woman doesn't like anyone."

She took Laurel's hand in a friendly handshake. "That would be wonderful, Laurel. I'm not familiar with

68

the styles out west. I've just come from Scotland with my husband, Killian." *It wasn't exactly a lie.* "If you could make suggestions, I'd be grateful."

Laurel took out a sketch pad and flipped a few pages. "Here are a few styles I like. Simple yet elegant." She gave Chinoah an appraising look.

"I don't want anything too fussy or uncomfortable to wear. You understand?"

"Sure. I feel the same." Laurel flipped a couple more pages and waved her hand over a design with lace at the bottom of bell sleeves, a slightly fitted bodice with a soft scalloped neckline. The full but not puffy skirt draped a woman's figure, with matching scalloped edges at the hemline.

"I love the way this type of dress swishes when you walk, with the right material. I was thinking of light rust with burnished yellow accents at the waist and cuffs of your sleeves. The color would highlight your beautiful skin tone."

"Sounds delightful. I like the design, so let's go with it."

"Wonderful. It's my design." Laurel said proudly. "Mrs. Lowery didn't like it but didn't say I couldn't show it to customers. You'd be the first in town with the design. I hope that's all right." The woman worried the edge of her jacket, then glanced up at Chinoah.

"No problem. I like to be a trendsetter." She pulled at her jeans and sweater.. "Comfortable and serviceable when you work in a blacksmith shop. A style most ladies disapprove of." She laughed. "However, my husband approves, and he doesn't have to keep replacing expensive dresses that get filthy, or the hems get ripped or torn."

Laurel smiled uncertainly. "Most women wouldn't or couldn't perform the job you do."

"I happened into it when Killian's former shop got so busy he didn't have time to do the bookkeeping. You know he makes swords, daggers, and repairs guns in addition to the usual blacksmith fare. Great with horses too. If you are ever in need. Heard Caleb is the man to see about a horse. Right?"

"Yes. Caleb's been a horse rancher forever. I saw him talking to your husband." Laurel glanced at the door. "I better be going. My son will be wondering after me."

"So nice to meet you. Glad you stopped by. I was planning on searching for the dress shop tomorrow."

"Let me take a few measurements." Laurel took out her measuring tape. "I'll let you know when I have the dress ready for fitting. Probably the first part of next week." Laurel finished with the measurements, waved as she opened the door, and walked out into the shop.

*Well, now that was unexpected but saved me traipsing into the dress shop unannounced.* She followed Laurel and glanced out the door at Killian. He met her gaze, raised an eyebrow, and mouthed, "You okay?"

"Fine," she replied in kind." Her self-confidence restored, she stepped out into the forge. "Need any help?" She put her hand on his arm.

He leaned over and brushed a kiss on her cheek. "Nope, got it handled—or just about." He laughed, shifting his glance to Luke, who was still dealing with a demanding customer. "Think that's another job that Joe didn't get completed." He patted her hand. "I better go offer a discount and see if we can't smooth over the situation."

"Good luck." She wandered back into her office. At

her desk, she opened the ledgers left by Joe. *What a mess.* At least he had a comprehensive customer list, listing their preferences and usual orders, including notes on cantankerous horses and owners. Leaning back in her chair, she snickered. Mrs. Chambers even made Joe's list and not in a good way. The records also indicated Caleb and Joe had gotten crosswise about horseshoeing. She made a note to bring that to Killian's attention if Caleb hadn't and finished her review of the ledgers.

Killian knocked on the door frame to her office. "Hey pretty lady, ready to go home with me?" He gave her a slow seductive smile.

"Guess so. You handsome bloke." She pushed up from her chair, slid the ledgers into the top desk drawer and locked it. "The books tell an interesting story. You might want to take a look to avoid a situation like you just handled. Apparently, Joe was a bit difficult after he got sick, but before he left. There are several unfinished projects with side notes indicating he didn't intend to finish their projects. He also had a problem with Caleb. He's the horse rancher that married Laurel, if you didn't know."

The woman who came to visit you?" Killian walked to her and wrapped his big hands around her waist and pulled her to him. "Aye, Caleb and I discussed Joe. You smell fantastic." He inhaled deeply. "I love that lilac shampoo you use." He thought a minute. "I like the citrus one too. So fresh. Like you. And forbidden."

"Yep." Laughing, she snuggled against him. "Anything would smell good after working in the forge all day." She wrinkled her nose. "Did you get the situation handled?"

He rested his cheek on the top of her head. "Yep.

Deep discount on the customer's item that is late and lesser discount on his next order. Luke will have his late order done and delivered to him by the end of next week." Leaning back, he tilted his head, eyebrow raised. "The woman?"

"Oh—Laurel, she's a seamstress at Lowery's Dress Shoppe and Laundry. Cissy told her I might be interested in a gown for the Harvest and Christmas Balls. Guess Cissy didn't trust that I had formal clothes." She giggled. "And she'd be right. Anyway, Laurel brought designs and had suggestions for the gowns."

"And…"

"Your wallet is going to be a lot lighter. I ordered a Harvest Ball gown. After I see how the fitting goes next week, I'll probably order a Christmas one too. Not too fancy or sexy but elegant and comfortable to wear. It'll swish when I walk."

"Did you bring jewelry to compliment your gowns?" He grinned.

"You know the answer to that. I don't have any jewelry to compliment anything." She glanced down at the plain gold band on the all-important finger of her left hand. "Except this fake wedding ring," she whispered the last words.

"Ouch. Nothing fake about it. It's a superior gold band with a promise." He winced, returning her whisper. Changing the subject, he released her and reached for her coat. "You ready to head to the cabin? Swiped some popcorn and butter from Luke. Figured it'd be a nice night to sit in front of the fireplace and eat popcorn. After dinner, of course."

She slid her arms in the coat he held for her, pulled pink gloves, a matching knit hat, and scarf out of the pockets, and put them on. "Fireplace doesn't work. It's drafty. Come on, Adventure. You're not staying here tonight. There's a nice warm cabin waiting for us." She bent down and clipped a leash on the dog's new harness. Addy tugged on it, sat down, scratched on the harness, and promptly chewed on the leash.

"Don't think she likes that setup. Probably been on her own to wander around at will." He glanced at the pup.

Luke glanced at them with a smirk. "You'd be exactly right. Dog's never had a collar or leash. Followed Joe everywhere. Pup probably knows this town better than most."

"It's a new day. Don't want her getting hurt or lost." Chinoah looked down at the dog. "Isn't that right, girl? Besides, you won't be staying here all the time. We've got places to go."

Resigned, Addy finally gave a shake and stood in place staring dejectedly up at her.

"It'll be fine. You'll see."

"On a happier note, I plan to fix the fireplace." He shrugged into his coat and hat. "I love a good roaring fire for cuddling with my woman. Wood stoves are all right but lack a certain ambiance. Don't you agree?"

"Ambiance is hard to create when you're freezing." She tossed him a saucy smile.

"We banked the stoves when we left, so should take the chill off." He twined his gloved fingers with hers and left the forge. "Night Luke. Thanks for the popcorn."

"Anytime." Luke crossed the room and closed the door behind them.

Killian snapped his fingers. "We should detour to the telegraph office. I need to answer the shaman's telegram. He didn't sign it, so I don't even know his name, only that he is up north in what the Native Americans call Healing Waters on the far northeast side of the Shoshone Reservation. Want to arrange a meet with him as soon as possible."

"The telegraph office is all the way at the end of Old Cheyenne Road in the opposite direction as our cabin. We need a couple of horses and carriage," she complained.

"I'll see what I can do about that. Right now, think how physically fit you'll be by the time this assignment is over." He laughed and dodged her hand.

\*\*\*\*

A fast-paced walk to the telegraph office, then to the cabin, got the blood pumping. By the time he opened the cabin door, the wind had started to kick up again. "Does the wind always blow around here?" She stepped inside and took off her gloves, hat, and scarf.

"That's what I've heard. A guy at the newspaper said the next few days were supposed to be much nicer. Might even melt the snow, and no wind to speak of is forecast."

"I'll believe that when I see it." She walked to the icebox and peered inside. "What do you want for dinner?" When she turned around, the table was set, candles lit, and two covered dishes that smelled like heaven were arranged in the center. Mugs of hot chocolate steamed next to the place settings and a bottle of wine chilled at the end of the table. "Where did all this come from?"

"A little angel magic after a few exceptionally rough days won't tip the scales of using magic for personal gain." He smiled and reached for her. "I appreciate your efforts and not complaining—too much."

"You owe me big time." She stared at the table. "But this really helps. I'm starved." Shrugging out of her coat, she was surprised at how warm it was in the cabin.

"Me too." He took her coat, slipped out of his, and hung both on the hooks near the front door. Escorting her over to the table, he pulled a chair out. "Have a seat."

"Why, thank you, kind sir." She eased into the chair and beamed up at him.

"Of course. I treat my woman well." He plopped into a chair across from her, then got up moved the chair beside her.

"What's all this "my woman" stuff? I'm not property," she said indignantly.

"You slap at me when I call you my wife, even when we are alone. You aren't anyone else's woman. Are you?"

She shook her head. *Where he's going with this?*

"Consequently, it stands to reason that you're my woman." A smug smile curved his full luscious lips.

She loved the feel of his soft, warm lips on hers. A sigh escaped her lips at the thought. "Given your reasoning, you'd be my man. Correct?"

"Exactly." The corners of his eyes crinkled with delight as his brilliant blue eyes sparkled with mischief. He picked up the lid to the first pan. Pork chops and stuffing smothered in a cream sauce simmered. He forked out a chop for each, then added stuffing and covered it all with the sauce.

"Oh, that smells fantastic and looks even better." She watched as he took the lid off the second dish. Berry cobbler bubbled through a crispy topping of cinnamon crumble. Her very favorite. "Okay, I admit, you spoil me." She breathed in the steaming cobbler as her mouth watered. "After all this, I don't see how we'll have room for popcorn."

"The night is young." A devilish smile spread across his face.

She cut the chop into pieces and popped one in her mouth. "Mmmmm, this is so good."

With meat on his fork, he slid it through the sauce and added a bit of stuffing. "Hits the spot on a cold night."

They finished dinner, put the dishes in the sink and took their wine into the living room. Easing onto the couch in front of the roaring fire, he swirled the burgundy liquid in his glass. The wine shimmered.

"Hey." She held out a hand toward the fire as she passed by him. "No cold draft like this afternoon." She blinked and glanced back at him. "Did you have something to do with that?"

"You could say that." He chuckled. "An angel never reveals his secrets."

She rubbed her hands together, warming them by the fire. "Really. Not even going to ask. Assume you know what you're doing. It's nice." Cuddled up next to him, she took a sip of her wine. "This is extraordinary. Fruity, fresh, and a fragrant bouquet." She picked up the bottle and studied it. "Why no label?"

"Angel stock." His lips twitched before he finally chuckled at her astonished expression. "Only kidding. I grabbed it from my cousin's stash before we left Scotland. Tavish is a wine connoisseur and stocks only the best. And before you ask, he doesn't mind sharing." Setting his glass on the coffee table, he leaned over and brushed his lips over hers, his tongue tracing the fullness of her lips.

She gave herself freely to the passion of his kiss, sending her stomach into a wild swirl of desire. Her mind warned her to stop. Her traitorous body refused to listen. The wine was tart on his lips, mixed with the sweet berry cobbler from supper was a pleasant combination. She slipped deeper into the kiss as his hands roamed over her heated body.

As he kissed down her neck and began to unbutton her blouse, she reluctantly put her hand on top of his. Her heart beating a tattoo in her chest as moisture gathered in her nether regions. "I don't think either of us is ready to follow this path we're headed down."

"Speak for yourself," he murmured, his lips against her breast, tongue teasing beneath her bra.

"I am. If I understand the angel rules correctly, if we consummate our relationship with intimacy we are bound to each other for eternity."

He sat upright. "True." He slipped his fingers beneath her waistband. "But there's a little wiggle room. We can pleasure each other without…"

She shook her head. "Could you stop once you started? Are you sure?" Pausing, she closed her eyes and blew out a frustrated breath. "If it's for eternity, I want to make sure it's right. Don't you?"

He was silent for several beats. His seductive blue eyes smoldered with desire. "Of course, but I'm still a man with all the needs that go along with it."

"Shouldn't get yourself aroused. You don't believe I have the same needs? Especially when you're teasing me."

"Oh, I had a little help in the arousal department. As I said—I can satisfy your needs without…" His voice trailed off as his mouth returned to her breasts and his fingers flipped open the buttons on her jeans.

Her mind screamed stop, yet her legs spread, allowing him access. His magic fingers had her lost in a sexual haze of desire. Caresses felt so good. She let her head loll back and gave him complete access for whatever came next. Her wine glass slipped from her fingers and shattered on the floor. The sexual haze cleared. "We can't do this, Killian." Jumping up, she began to clean up the broken glass.

He growled, easing her away from the glass. "Let me do that before you cut yourself."

"What, you don't think I've cleaned up glass before? Without injury."

"Didn't say that. It's my fault. You're right. But it doesn't mean I like it. Our arrangement is going to drive me crazy."

"Then you might want to get on your assignment sooner than later." Slowly she buttoned her blouse and zipped up her jeans. Still, desire circled in her belly while she helped him clean up the mess. *Would it really be so bad to allow him to...* Again her mind struggled with her mutinous body. After mopping up the spilled wine, she turned to him. "You take the master bedroom. I'll take the small one. Sharing a bed is not in either of our best interests."

"Fine." He banked the fire in the fireplace, added logs to the stove, and stalked off in the direction of the master bedroom.

Adventure yawned, rolled over, and curled up again in front of the fire.

Chapter Eight

Mysterious Telegram Followed by An Unusual Visitor

Picking several logs out of the pile, Chinoah carried them to the small bedroom. As she suspected, there was no supply of wood in the room. Thank goodness there was a wood-burning stove in all the rooms. *Our perfectly wonderful day is in ruins. My fault.* She washed up, brushed her hair, and slipped the cozy flannel gown over her still tingling body.

*Damn him.* She jerked the covers over her head, punched her pillow, and let sleep flow over her. Erotic dreams of Killian filled her night, making her more tired and irritable than she'd been the night before.

The aroma of freshly brewed coffee and sizzling bacon wafted into the room. She jumped out of bed. Stomped over to her clothes from last night, slung over the back of a wooden chair, and guilt reared its ugly head. Wearing those clothes wasn't an option but going into his bedroom to retrieve clean clothes wasn't a good idea either. *How is this ever going to work?*

She cracked the door just a little. The path clear, she tiptoed down the hall to his bedroom, then paused to listen. A sigh of relief left her lips. He was still in the kitchen. Padding over to the closet, she silently slid open the door. A wide array of everyday dresses, blouses, sweaters, skirts, including the requested jeans, riding breeches and aprons in bright colors hung on rods. Shoes she'd seen the other women wearing lined the floor.

Men's attire hung on the other side with a few pairs of different types of boots. She glanced at the dresser. *What do you suppose are in those drawers? Brought enough underwear to last a while.* The clanging of pans came from the kitchen. She grabbed jeans and a sweater, then scurried back to her room. Once safely inside, she closed the door.

Her thoughts returned to the previous night, then to when he'd healed her after the fiasco in Riverton, Wyoming the previous year. He'd never made these kinds of advances even though they laid naked together during the process, his wings folded around her. Later as they grew closer, he'd explained to her what happened when an angel fell in love and consummated that relationship.

There was no denying the spark of attraction that zinged between them. They'd agreed to take it slow, even discussing the possible pitfalls of spending the holidays in Scotland. He convinced her it was the next step in their relationship.

Then *bam, s*he threw up her hands. Here they were in 1878, masquerading as a married couple without the benefits. Surprised, she discovered she wanted those benefits. *Maybe I'm overthinking it. Is he the one? I gotta be sure. Eternity is a long time.*

Idly she wondered how that worked between an immortal and a shapeshifter? *Probably the reason such relationships were forbidden by the Angel Tribunal initially. Then along came Caden and Mystic challenging the rules.*

When she and Killian became involved, Killian, Caden, Nat, and Mystic had been emphatic in telling her there was no divorce in a marriage to an angel. Her best friend, Mystic's words rang in her ears "better be sure." Shrugging, she opened the door, and her stomach growled loudly. She bounced to the kitchen.

Scrambled eggs were in a skillet on the stove, and bacon still sizzled on a plate on the table. Steaming mugs of coffee sat next to the dishes. Adventure greeted her with a wagging tail and nudged her hand to be petted. She scratched the dog behind the ears and leaned down. "Abandoned me last night, didn't you?"

The dog tilted her head up in what appeared to be puzzlement.

"Never mind, we'll discuss it later." Running her fingers over the dog's tail that curved over her back she vowed silently to give the dog a brushing and bath this weekend, weather permitting.

Killian waved a utensil toward the table. "Have a seat." He divided the eggs between the two plates, returned the pan to the stove, and plopped down in the chair next to hers. "About last night…"

"Forget it."

"No. I was thinking with body parts other than my brain. You're right. Sorta. We need to be sure, but if you ever want me to—uh— scratch that itch for you, I'm all in." His wild, wicked blue eyes surveyed every inch of her. "As I said, there are ways around the requirement—that is until you—uh—we're ready."

"Good to know." She ignored the tingles his stare caused, took a bite of bacon, and chewed thoughtfully. "I was to blame as much as you." She admitted. "We need to keep our emotions on a low simmer."

"Easy for you to say. Males aren't built that way. At least I wasn't."

"Wait a minute, how many mortal women did you bed?" She squared her shoulders.

"Um…not really sure." He scrubbed his hand over his face. "But I can assure you that none of them mattered until you."

"So you took advantage of them?"

"No, no, it was mutual satisfaction, then they went on their way, as did I. As long as neither party had feelings for the other, the sexual act had no consequences. You can't believe a male several hundred years old could exist without—release."

"How would I know?" she shot back. "In my world, angels are—were perfect. Until a year ago, there was no division between what you call goody two shoes white fluffy angels and the tough battle-ready warrior angels—with needs." She snorted.

"Time to table this discussion. We need to get to town and to work. We got this. Last night was a little hiccup. Fair enough." His face beamed with the charming smile she couldn't resist.

"Okay. I reserve the right to revisit the conversation if you bring the heat again."

"Whoa, wait a minute. Heat flowed both ways, lass." He gave a low chuckle and caressed her arse, then sprinted into his bedroom.

****

The streets were quiet in the early morning. The sun shone brightly, and no breeze. They strolled on the sidewalks pausing to peer into the shop windows on the way. Adventure trotted beside them.

"Much more pleasant than yesterday." She pulled

her hat and scarf off, enjoying the warm sun on her face before entering the shop door Killian held for her. "I'm going to catch up on the bookkeeping from yesterday, then head over to the dress shop or bakery and ask Cissy or Laurel where I might purchase lingerie in this town." Turning to hang her coat on the hooks, she saw Luke standing there, his face scarlet.

"You're in early, she huffed. "Well, you do know we wear such things?"

Killian smiled before leaning down and kissing her affectionately on the lips, lingering for a moment. "Quit teasing the help darl'n, and I'd try Cissy first. Laurel's boss, widow Lowery, can be a bit crotchety when it comes to taking up the time of her staff during work hours."

"Look at you, talking like you've known these people for years," Chinoah teased.

"Learned a lot from listening to men talk yesterday." Killian moved to slap Luke on the back. "Shall we get to work?"

"Yes, sir."

"We discussed this. It's Killian."

Luke nodded. A shy grin danced around his lips.

"Killian, you should talk to Caleb about buying a horse or two. Would he know where to buy a carriage?" She batted her eyes and smiled coyly at him.

"Look at you, spending money before we've earned it." He grinned back at her. "Seriously, I'll look into it. We'll have to make arrangements for the horses here and at the cabin. I didn't see a barn on the property."

Luke opened his mouth, then shut it again and followed Killian across the room.

Chinoah ambled to her office with Adventure

trotting beside her. Rounding the desk, she sat and pulled out the ledgers. Two hours later, she emerged from the office, the dog trailing behind her. "Killian?"

"Over here." He straightened next to the anvil that Luke still bent over, measuring a large piece of steel.

She sauntered across the forge toward the men. "I've counted the money received yesterday, credited it to the correct accounts, and the deposit is ready. Addy and I are going to the bank and run a few errands. Need anything?"

"Nope." He turned to look at Luke. "You?"

"No. I'm going over to Jilly's after work."

"Good enough, I'll see you two later. Come along Addy." She took her coat, hat, and scarf from the hooks by the door.

He came up behind her, helped her on with the coat, and kissed her before pulling her close. "Hurry back." Reaching for the door handle, he opened the door and stepped out with her. "Sunshine feels good. Believe we'll call it a day an hour early, so if you're not back by then, I'll find you, and we'll walk to the cabin together. Tomorrow I have a meeting with Caleb to see about horses. Caleb claims to have an old carriage that needs repair he's willing to sell to us for a fair price."

"Fantastic. I'll be back." She waved and walked down the sidewalk, the dog trailing behind.

He closed the door and went back to work. Sometime later, the door creaked open, and a tall man with long straight black hair in two braids down his back entered. "I'm looking for Killian Dugan."

"You found him. Who might you be?" Killian extended his hand.

The man shook the hand. "Raymond Swiftwater. I

sent you a telegram a few days back. Decided to discuss it with you in person when I learned you'd arrived."

"Wow, news travels fast around here."

The skin around the man's eyes crinkled when he grinned. "Spirit wind misses nothing."

"You came all the way from Healing Waters? That's quite a trip."

"I had business in a few towns along the way. Sent the telegram from Fort McKinney. I'll be staying at Culpepper's. Where can I get a good hot meal?" Raymond took off his hat and tapped it against his leg. Dust rose in a cloud then sifted to the floor.

"You'll do no such thing. We have a spare room at our cabin and more than enough food. I'm waiting for Chinoah to return from errands, and we'll walk to the cabin. It's not far." He turned toward Luke and introduced him to Raymond. "We're going to shut down early today. The other projects will wait until tomorrow." He waggled his eyebrows. "More time to spend with Jilly."

"Thank you, sir, uh, Killian." He nodded toward Raymond. "Good to meet you, sir."

Raymond returned his hat to his head and nodded. "Yes."

Chinoah burst through the door with packages swinging from her arms and the dog at her heels. "Wait until you see…" She skidded to a halt a couple of feet from the visitor, shifting her gaze from Killian to the stranger. The dog nearly ran into her leg, sniffed the air, then barked. "Quiet, Addy."

A grin spread across Killian's face. "My effervescent wife, Chinoah, our dog Adventure, this is Raymond Swiftwater. He's the shaman from Healing

Waters and has information on our assignment."

Addy quickly lost interest and trotted over to her rug, circled twice and settled by the stove.

Chinoah's eyes rounded. "Already? Didn't you just send…"

"Raymond didn't receive my telegram. He was traveling this way when he heard we were here."

"Oh. How—Never mind."

"I've invited him to stay with us before starting his trip back home. He'll be joining us for supper, so we better be on our way. We can warm up the leftovers from last night."

She hugged her packages to her chest. "If you say so."

He blew out the lamps and banked the coals in the forge. "Shall we?" He pulled open the door, whistled for Addy, and waited for Chinoah and Raymond to exit. Closing the door behind him, he locked it and pocketed the key. "How was your shopping trip?"

"It was productive. Cissy had some suggestions and…" She held up a box tied with string. "A surprise for dessert."

He snatched the box from her and inhaled deeply, tipping the box so Raymond could see. "A lemon chiffon pie. I've not had one of those—in several years. Yum." Offering to carry her other packages, he reached for them.

"Oh no. I'll take the bakery box. You take the rest of the packages. Did you have ice delivered?"

"I did. We didn't need as much as I thought."

"We need to think about Christmas decorations. I guess we'll have to make our own this year. Caleb and Laurel are having a holiday get together at the ranch.

We're invited." She paused. "I told her we'd be there."

"Funny, Luke and I were just talking about doing the same thing at the forge. It's warm in there. We could clean it up and…"

"Stop right there. No one will want to eat food in the forge. If you want to do a holiday bash, we'll have to do it at the cabin. If we have a carriage by then, we could decorate it all up with holly and pine boughs. Then offer carriage rides around the property." A mischievous smile curved her lips and sparkled in her eyes. "Can you build a sleigh?"

"I s'pose I could. What ya thinking?"

"I've always wanted to go on a sleigh ride with friends. Have hot cocoa, popcorn and sing Christmas Carols. Wouldn't that be fun?"

"I think we better see how welcoming everyone is at the Harvest Ball. I don't want you disappointed after working hard on a party, and no one comes. Besides, the church or community may have festivities too."

Raymond glanced at Chinoah. "What tribe do you belong? If you don't mind me asking."

"Kinda hard to explain, but my mom was Eastern Shoshone, and dad was Northern Arapaho." She shrugged. "And you?"

He raised an eyebrow then nodded slowly. "Interesting joining. Those tribes were bitter enemies until they were forced to live on the reservation together in 1869. All accounts claim it was amicable, but it wasn't. Isn't. Was it a willing… Never mind, none of my business. My wife and I are Eastern Shoshone."

"We're here." Killian unlocked the door and pushed it open. Addy was first through the door, rushed to her blanket between the fireplace and the couch. "Feels like the fires went out, didn't bank them well enough this morning. Still getting used to—a cabin of this size."

He stoked the wood stoves and piled logs high on the fireplace. "It'll warm up quickly." He and Chinoah walked into the kitchen. He took the covered dishes from last night out of the icebox. Stoked the fire in the cooking stove, then slid the pans inside.

In a whisper, she said, "We ate everything in those dishes last night. What are you up to, Killian Dugan?"

In a quiet voice, he continued, "Unless you want to spend the next several hours cooking, we'll have leftovers of pot roast, with potatoes, carrots, and the dessert you brought. I'm exhausted. Forging is hard work and meant for the young. I can't believe how Luke puts out the projects."

"Sounds good to me. More angel magic?"

"This gentleman has information for our investigation. So using a bit of magic to make him feel at home falls under my category of necessary angel magic."

"You justify it any way you want. You'll be answering to Nat, not me." She flounced out to join their guest in the living area. Raymond stood in front of the fireplace as it snapped and popped from the sap in the wood. "You can sit anywhere. Killian will be along shortly. He likes to build up the fires in all the stoves to keep the cabin cozy and warm."

"I'll stand. Thank you. Traveling takes more sitting than I'm accustomed. This is a beautiful home."

"Thank you. We like it." She plopped down on the couch. "Tell me about Healing Waters."

"It's due north of here about three hundred miles. It's a long trip, which is why I plan many stops along the way if I must rely on conventional travel. Rumor has it that Chief Washakie is considering giving the white man our Healing Waters. I'm opposed."

"Doesn't sound like a smart thing." Killian came back into the room. Raymond was still standing beside the fireplace.

Killian eased down beside Chinoah. "No disrespect, but I've been on my feet all day. I need to get off them for a while." He took his boots off, wiggled his toes, and placed the footwear on the woven mat beside the couch.

"None taken. As I explained to your wife, traveling requires me to sit more than I like." Raymond chuckled.

"Think he regrets allowing the Northern Arapaho on the Shoshone Reservation?"

"Don't think he had a choice. It's long a story. I'm weary and want to tell you why I'm here."

Chapter Nine

Good or Evil Only Time Will Tell, but Things May Not be as They Appear

"Okay. Shoot."

"No, wait a minute. Let's eat supper while he tells us." Chinoah got to her feet and padded into the kitchen, motioning Raymond and Killian to follow.

She lit the lamps in the kitchen. Shadows from the flames danced on the cabin walls. It only took her a few minutes to take the heated pans out of the oven and arrange them on the table.

The cocoa in a pan on top of the stove was warm as well. Killian took the pan and poured the steaming liquid into mugs and set them by each plate. Taking a large spoon, fork, and carving knife out of the drawer, she handed the knife to Killian. He removed the lid from the meat dish and sliced the roast. She placed the spoon and fork in the pan so everyone could serve themselves. The other pan was full of cornbread. Killian cut it into square pieces.

Once everyone was seated around the table and their plates were full, Raymond began.

"The whispering spirits of the Healing Waters have been disturbed by an interloper from another world, time, or dimension. They feel evil intentions but are unable to trace or locate the creature. He corrupts the timeline each time he moves around. The spirits are very concerned." He buttered the cornbread and bit into it closed his eyes. "Very good."

Killian forked up a piece of roast. "So why come to me?" He pointed the fork at Raymond.

The shaman stopped his fork of potato halfway to his mouth. "Why you. I'm not here to play games. I know who and what you are, including why you and your wife are here. I want to soothe the spirits before—things get out of hand."

"You have me at a disadvantage. I don't know who you are other than a Shoshone shaman, which obviously may be true, but how do I know you aren't the creature I'm searching for?" Killian leveled a steely gaze at the shaman and scooped up a bite of potato and carrot.

"Excellent question. My visions tell me what travels I need to keep peace in the valley. I can take many forms in my visions but am only a Shoshone shaman on this plane of existence. In my visions, the spirits told me to seek out the one traveling with a shapeshifter and that you could help me. I have no other proof that I am who I say I am, other than had I been the creature you seek, I'd have killed you by now and been on my way."

"Good point. Is this creature's movements random, or is there a pattern?" He took a bite of his buttered cornbread.

"So far as I can tell, random. He appears at the reservation about once a month. Stays a couple of days, then is gone. Also, the railroad on the reservation seems to interest him. The train station in Wylder is also where he was spotted."

"Is he a creature of the full moon?"

"No. Better to sneak around the rez without being

seen with less moonlight. The rez is not a safe place for outsiders in our time."

"Not in our time either." Chinoah grimaced, wiping her plate with her last piece of cornbread. "Better now with steady enforcement, but still a dangerous place."

"Sorry to hear that. I'd hoped for better as the years went on." A wide yawn caught the shaman by surprise. "If you'd show me to my room, I'd like to go to sleep now. Perhaps the spirits may have more to tell me tonight."

"Of course." He shoved to his feet showed Raymond to his room. When he returned, Chinoah had cleared the table and put all the dishes in the sink. "What do you think?"

"I think he's a time traveler too." She said, "Besides having the sight to talk with the spirits. I believe he is who he says he is and that the spirits want this demon caught as bad as Nat and the Angel Tribunal."

"So you buy his story?" He studied her as she took wine glasses out of the cupboard. "Why don't we take the wine and relax in front of the fire? These wooden chairs need padding."

Without hesitation, she nodded. "Yes. Don't you believe him? And you are so right about these chairs."

After pouring the wine into glasses and handing her one, he eased down on the sofa and patted the place beside him. "Mighty convenient timing on his part." He rolled his shoulders.

She took a sip of her glass and set it on the table, reached over, and massaged his shoulders. "What other reason would he be here and tell us that story?"

"I don't know. The warrior in me always distrusts something that seems too easy." He took a long sip of his wine. "This hits the spot."

She swirled the burgundy liquid in the glass, watched it sparkle in the firelight and yawned. "I think Raymond had the right idea."

He caught her hand, brought it to his cheek, turned his head, and kissed her palm. "You have to share my bed tonight."

She narrowed her eyes at him. "I what?" Pausing, she lifted an eyebrow. "Oh yes, we have company. Guess you'll be sleeping on the floor tonight."

"After the day I've had, no way. We'll share the bed. It's not like we sleep naked." He hesitated as a wicked grin tipped up one corner of his mouth. "Do you?"

"In your dreams," she shot back.

"Not what I had in mind. But right now, I'm too tired to care." He finished off his wine and took her hand. "Shall we? Thanks for the massage. It helped."

"My poor angel doesn't have the stamina he used to have." She snickered.

"Oh, I wouldn't say that. Care to make a little wager?" He beetled his eyebrows.

She snatched her hand away. "I wasn't talking about that, and you know it."

He sighed. "One can always hope." He carried the glasses and wine into the kitchen, then laced his fingers through hers as they ambled to their bedroom. He shut the door, turned to lean down, and caressed her lips with his. She resisted for only a beat, then wrapping her arms around his neck and parting her lips, she raised on tiptoe to deepen the kiss.

****

He woke up to the sound of running water. Jerking to a sitting position in bed, he rubbed his eyes. Chinoah's side of the bed was empty.

She walked out of the bathroom, toweling her hair. Steam billowed out into the chilly room. "Wanted to get an early start to the morning. When I talked with Crissy, she had a message from Laurel to come by the dress shop for a fitting of my Harvest Ball gown."

"It's done already?"

She huffed out a laugh. "No. But she needs to check the fit and the length."

"Oh." He tumbled out of bed in his pajama bottoms. "How'd you sleep?"

"Good. And you?"

"Great. I had a beautiful woman beside me." He tossed logs in the wood stove on his way to the bathroom.

"With bedclothes and pj's between us." She said primly.

"There was that." He laughed. "Would you throw a few small logs in the kitchen and living area stoves? I'll be right along to stoke 'em up good."

"Sure. How was business yesterday?" Slipping into vintage jeans out of her closet, she pulled on a new spring green sweater. "I'll get breakfast started. Our guest is probably starved. I know I am." She sat on the side of the bed to put shoes and socks on.

"Steady. Took in several payments as well. You'll be busy at the forge for the first part of the day." Dressed in jeans and a blue plaid shirt, he emerged from the bathroom. Quiet footsteps in the hall outside the bedroom sounded. "Must be Ray."

She opened the door. "Good morning, Ray. I'll be right down to start breakfast."

The shaman paused. "Good morning. I'll be on my way today."

"Not before you've had breakfast." She shook a finger at him.

"Don't want to trouble you. I'm sure there's a place to eat in town," he said easily.

\*\*\*\*

"Sure is, and there's a place to eat here. Have a seat. I'll have breakfast ready in a jiffy." Chinoah bounded out the bedroom door and into the kitchen. *Shit. I forgot I have to stoke wood in the cookstove before cooking.* "Well, maybe a bit longer. But you're not leaving here on an empty stomach," she called out, pausing to fill Adventure's water and food bowl. The men followed her to the kitchen.

Killian nodded in agreement.

Ray smiled. "Thank you. Can I help with anything?"

"If you don't mind. Help Chinoah get the cooking stove going while I stoke the other stoves will speed up breakfast. A bit chilly in here this morning."

"Of course. It'll take a while to get used to the way of life here—in Wyoming." The shaman met Killian's gaze with a knowing look.

"I won't argue. Bet you know better than most." Killian returned the man's gaze.

Ray smiled and simply nodded, picking up three logs and dropping them into the stove's firebox. Arranging several pieces of kindling between the logs with his back to them, he appeared to wave a hand over the wood, and it sparked to life in a big way.

"Shouldn't be long now." His smile broadened, and amusement showed, the skin around his eyes crinkling while he leveled a gaze at Killian. "I've many talents of the shaman learned from my father and his father before him and so on. Using them while I travel is convenient

95

and eases the way of life in this Wyoming Territory."

"Understood." He took orange juice out of the icebox and poured it in glasses Chinoah had set on the table. "Last of the juice."

She poured coffee in mugs. "Cream or sugar?"

"Black. Thanks." His brow creased. "Why don't you two come on up to Healing Waters in a few weeks. Spend a few days. My wife, Lily, loves company. I may have more information for you by that time. The waters will calm your shoulder and back. Blacksmithing is hard physical work."

"Sounds like a plan." Killian rolled his shoulders. "We'll do that. I'll send word when we plan to leave Wylder."

Bacon sizzled, filling the room with its aroma as she scooped scrambled eggs onto their plates. She forked the bacon onto a plate and set it in the center of the table. "Help yourselves." She paused to sip orange juice before settling down at the table. She mulled over the conversation, more confident than ever he was a time traveler.

"This is delicious. Much obliged." Ray mopped up the remaining egg with his last piece of toast. Taking a big gulp of his coffee, he set the mug down. "Gotta get going. Thanks so much for the hospitality." He took his hat and coat off the pegs by the front door. "See ya soon."

She cleared off the table, Killian helped with the dishes, and they were ready to go to work. Donning coats, hats, and gloves, they opened the door to bright sunshine and blue sky. Her brightly colored scarf wrapped around her neck, she drew her coat closer around her as the wind tugged at it. Adventure trotted along beside them, except for the occasional need to chase a rabbit or other small furry creature.

She shivered. "The sunshine is deceiving." The brisk walk to Dugan's got her heart pumping and warming everything but her feet. "I believe I need some different boots." She stomped her feet, knocking the mud off before entering the forge.

"Or thicker socks." Killian teased.

"Or both. If I had a horse and/or carriage my boots wouldn't be a problem."

"We'll have to see about that. Not sure how Adventure will feel about that."

"She'll get used to it." Stopping in front of the roaring fireplace, she took off her outerwear and hung it on the iron stand with bars off to the side. "Brilliant idea to add these free-standing bars far enough from the fireplace to be safe but close enough to warm the cloth."

"It was Joe's idea," Luke called from across the room. "He always complained about the bone-chilling winter cold in recent years. Liked his coat and things warmed before he left for the night."

"It's a great idea." she reiterated, strolling to her office. *It's nice the heat from the fireplace and forges penetrates every corner of the building.* Kneeling on the floor, she opened the safe, took out yesterday's receipts and payments. Spreading them out on the desk, she opened the desk drawer, took out the ledger, and flipped pages to the correct date. Entering yesterday's receipts and payments took most of the morning.

At noon, Killian leaned on the door frame. "Hey beautiful, want to go to lunch?"

"What did you have in mind, handsome?" She batted her long, thick, black eyelashes and skirted around the desk to kiss him quick and hard.

He touched a finger to his lips. "A quick bite at Jake's place." He grinned seductively. "Don't have time for anything else— right now." Eyebrows raised, Killian smiled. His deep blue eyes sparked with mischief. "Later."

"I'm game. Let's go." She pushed up from her chair to see Luke, his face red, shaking his head. When he saw her peering at him, he quickly looked away. She laughed. "We gotta quit embarrassing Luke."

"It's merely continuing education." Killian chuckled. "If he's old enough to be serious about Jilly, he's old enough to handle our innuendos." He spun around and stared at Luke, catching him by surprise.

"Whatever you say," Luke mumbled, walking to the icebox, taking out his lunch.

"Why don't you join us?" Killian asked. "We'll close shop for an hour. Put a sign on the door where we'll be in case of emergency."

Silent for several beats, Luke appeared to be weighing his options.

"Aw, come on Luke, I won't let Killian tease you anymore—today." She winked at him, and he blushed again. *Good grief, he's naive, or he's one hell of an actor.*

Luke took off his leather apron, washed his hands, and put his lunch back in the icebox. "Sounds good."

On the way, they stopped at the bank to drop off the deposit. Mr. Mountroy glanced over and frowned at her. "Came straight from the forge." She shrugged.

Upon their arrival at Jake's, there was only one table left. Appeared, the whole town had decided Jake's was the place to be for lunch. A few snide remarks and open stares, which she met with narrowed eyes, then a few women twittered quietly. *I've had about enough of this.* Tomorrow I'll remember to bring an *everyday skirt.*

As if reading her mind, Killian put an arm around her and pulled her in for a lingering kiss. "We'll give them something to talk about," he murmured against her ear.

Luke quickly placed his order when the waitress stopped at the table. They added their order to his and told her one ticket.

Waiting for their meal, Luke and Killian discussed current and past orders, as well as the business forecast for the coming week.

"Are you taking Jilly to the Harvest Ball?" she asked cheerfully.

"Yes," Luke said tentatively.

"Oh good, then we'll get to meet her." Killian grinned.

"Stop it, Killian." She turned to a panicked Luke. "He'll be on his best behavior. I promise." She winked at him and put her napkin in her lap.

"It's not me you should be worried about." Killian shot a sidewise glance at Chinoah. "She's the wild one."

Before another finger-pointing session could take place, the waitress brought their drinks. "Food will be up in a minute."

"Thanks." She tilted her head up at Killian and had the urge to stick her tongue out at him but changed her mind and kicked him under the table.

A group of cowboys swaggered into Jake's, took the table just vacated by a family. The men were loud and obnoxious. They whistled for the waitress. When she walked over, one of the men grabbed her arm and pulled her down, trying to steal a kiss. She slapped him hard across the face. "You're in the wrong place. Wylder Social Club is across the railroad tracks." The waitress glared at him, turned on her heel, and stalked off.

Killian started to push up from the table, but she put her hand on his arm. "Let someone else handle it. We're new in town and don't want to…"

The words were not entirely out of her mouth when a big burly man strode out of the kitchen and made a beeline for the table. "Is there a problem here, boys?"

"Nope. Just wanted to order food," one cowboy said with a sneer.

"If you want service, leave the horseplay outside, or you can leave." The burly man stood hands on hips.

"Come on boys. Let's leave." The older of the men shoved up from the table, knocking a chair over.

The burly man escorted the group out the door. On his way back to the kitchen, he patted the waitress on the shoulder.

Excitement over, the waitress brought their food. "Sorry about that. Sometimes the cowboys passing through town leave their manners where they came from."

"No need to apologize. Wasn't your fault. Lunch and a show." Killian quipped.

The waitress gave a tired smile and moved on to the next table. They finished their lunch without incident. Killian paid the bill, escorted Chinoah out the door, with Luke bringing up the rear. "You going to be all right?"

"I'm only going across the street. I'll be fine. Meet you back at the forge in a couple of hours." She walked toward Sidewinder Lane and Lowery's Dress Shoppe. Killian and Luke strode towards Dugan's. She turned and waved at Killian and Luke as she started to cross the street. The stagecoach charged up the road. She hurriedly returned to the sidewalk and waited to cross the street. Suddenly, two of the rowdy cowboys sandwiched her between them.

"How about we show this dirty squaw how a real lady dresses?" One man with shaggy blond hair grabbed hold of her arm.

"We don't have any proper clothes for a lady." The other man shrugged and cackled showing his yellowed teeth. His breath reeked of whiskey when he leaned into her. He grabbed her other arm and twisted.

She screamed, jerked free, then slammed her forehead into the second man's nose, ground the heel of her shoe into the arch of his foot. Then she whirled around to elbow him in the stomach. When he bent over, she slammed her fists on the back of his neck, shoving him into the dirt. The other man advanced on her, an evil grin spread across his face at his partner's demise. Without hesitation, she planted her boot in his groin. He doubled over but caught hold of a wooden post gasping for breath.

Catching her breath, she brushed her hands together and fisted them at her waist.

Killian and Luke came running and tackled the shaggy-haired man.

"That's no way to treat a lady," Killian growled as he punched the man in the face. The man fell to the ground out cold. "You all right?" Killian pulled her to him holding her tight.

She relaxed against him for a moment, then eased out of his grip. "Yes, a bit winded, but fine." She rubbed her throbbing forehead where a knot was starting to form and brushed the dust off her jeans as a crowd gathered in the street.

"So much for keeping a low profile." Killian chided, but smiled proudly.

Laurel and Mrs. Lowery emerged from the dress shop. Laurel rushed across the street. "What happened?"

She kicked at the cowboy out cold. "These boys bit off a little more than they could chew." She scoffed. "Now, how is my dress coming?"

"Uh… I'd like you to take a look at it if you feel up to it." Laurel peered at her, concern creasing her forehead.

"Sure. I was on my way to the dress shop when I was waylaid." She laughed.

Luke returned with the sheriff in tow. Again she had to explain what happened. Sheriff Hanson hauled the two cowboys to their feet and shoved them toward the jail.

"Luke, you go on back to the forge. I'm going to accompany my wife on the rest of her errands. Then we'll be back." Killian motioned his apprentice toward the blacksmith shop.

"Killian Dugan, you'll do no such thing. I'm fine." Chinoah started across the street with Laurel.

Killian said nothing but followed her across the street and into the dress shop. "Good day Mrs. Lowery." He took off his hat as he entered the shop.

Chinoah glared at him. "I said."

"And if you don't remember, there were five cowboys in Jake's. Only two are cooling their heels in jail. You're not walking alone anywhere." His tone was mild but firm. "I'll wait right here." He glanced at Mrs. Lowery.

"Fine with me." Widow Lowery hustled into the dress shop, leaving him standing in the entryway. She turned with a stern gaze. "You're not allowed upstairs."

"Understood." He leaned his large frame against the wall, hat in his hands, and waited.

Approximately thirty minutes later, Chinoah bounced down the stairs and right past him. "I want to stop and see Cissy."

"Unless you want baked goods for tomorrow, you might want to hold off. Tonight, we are having supper with the Holts at their ranch. Caleb has a couple of horses for riding and pulling a carriage I'd like to see. He's offered an old carriage. I need to see if it will work for our needs and if I can repair it."

She stopped and back-peddled. "Really?"

"Yep. How'd the fitting go?"

"It's perfect. Wait until you see it. The material is soft, and it drapes nicely around my body. The bell sleeves are elegant. The gown swishes when I move like Laurel said it would. The woman is a wizard with a sewing machine."

"I can't wait to see it on you. But we'd better get back to the forge. We're expected at the Holt's Ranch before dusk." Killian took her elbow and led her out of the shop.

She turned to wave at Laurel standing at the top of the stairs and Mrs. Lowery standing behind the dress shop's counter.

Chapter Ten

Gotta See a Man About a Horse or Two and Maybe a Carriage

Upon their return to Dugan's, outside tied to the hitching posts were two horses. "Great, we can't leave the shop until we know where those horses came from." Killian patted the black horse's neck as he passed by.

Chinoah stopped and rubbed the beautiful buckskin horse's cheek. "Who left you out here? It's closing time. Bet you're hungry. Be right back." She followed him into the forge and waited for Addy, who paused to check out the new horses, to meander into the building before closing the door.

Luke greeted them from across the floor. "Caleb stopped by. He left those two horses for you to ride over the ranch tonight. Claimed you're interested in buying a couple of horses. These two have a calm disposition, and strangers don't bother them, according to Caleb. Said he'd see you tonight."

"Convenient. It's a nice night for a ride. Since they come from his stable, they'll know their way home." He turned to Chinoah. "Up for an evening ride?"

"Sure. Need to change first. Got blood and dirt all over my brand new sweater. I should take the cleaning fee out of that man's hide."

"Didn't you already do that?" He snickered.

"Not nearly as much as he deserved. I was more concerned at that time about my hide than his. Before I noticed the blood on my sweater." She brushed at the stain. "Yuck." Then walked over to the sink and washed her hands.

"All right if I leave now boss? It was a good day, even if we closed for a couple of hours at lunch. I counted out the till, put the deposit in the safe, and the receipts on Chinoah's desk." Luke shifted from foot to foot.

"Go ahead. Got a hot date with Jilly?"

"Sort of. We're going over to her parents' house for dinner, then play cards. They beat us every time. If I didn't know better, I'd say they were cheating."

"Playing partners?"

"Yes, Jilly and I against her parents."

"Change up the players. Her parents may have been married so long they know what each other will do. That puts you and Jilly at a disadvantage." He chuckled.

"Never thought of that. But don't want to rock the boat either. They like me, and I want to keep it that way." Luke shrugged one shoulder.

"Don't blame you. Go on, get out of here." He made shooing motions with his hand then turned to Chinoah. "Ready to go?"

"Yes." She walked toward the office. "I want to put the receipts in the ledger so they don't get lost." She disappeared into the office for a few minutes. When she returned with her bag slung over her shoulder Adventure trotted behind her. He jiggled the door, then locked it.

She bent down and rubbed the dog's ears. "Now, you follow us at a safe distance to the cabin." Without hesitation, Chinoah checked the buckskin's cinches, untied the reins, grabbed hold of the horn, shoved her foot in the stirrup, and swung into the saddle. The leather made a chaffing sound as she settled in.

"Let's go, girl." She nudged the horse's sides with her heels. "Watch out for the pup." The horse wiggled its ears back and forth and started at a slow walk, almost as if waiting for Killian to mount and catch up.

Adventure thundered ahead of them a few yards, paused to glance back, then continued.

"Addy. You wait for us," Chinoah called sharply.

The dog slowed its pace until Chinoah and the horse caught up with her. Once Killian joined the group, Addy took off at a run toward the cabin. She looked longingly at the dog.

Her wistful expression wasn't lost on him. "Been a while since you've had a run on four paws. Huh?"

"Yep. Too dangerous. As you pointed out, don't know where the ranchers set traps. Going to remedy that situation tonight if we aren't at the ranch too long. Even if it's just outside around the cabin. I feel all twitchy."

"Understood. We'll call it an early night if at all possible. I'll accompany you. Wings need a bit of a stretch too." He rolled his shoulders. "If not, tomorrow night for sure."

At the cabin, Chinoah dismounted and sprinted to the door. "I'll only be a minute."

Jogging after her, he closed the door behind them. "Hey, you don't think I'm going to dinner like this." He pulled at his soot-smudged jeans and shirtsleeves. "Need to find a leather shop to make me chaps and a full jacket for the forge like Luke's got, or my clothes are going to be worn out within the month, with cinder holes and soot."

"I hear you talking. I'm in the bedroom. Come here

106

and talk to me." She shimmied out of her jeans and sweater. She soaked the stain on her sweater in the water basin in an attempt to rinse out the bloodstain. Quickly she flipped on the shower and rinsed the day's grime off. Sorting through their closet in her underwear, she found a heavy lilac plaid skirt with a matching lilac sweater. "Who picked out these clothes?"

"No idea." He stood in the doorway, arm raised and braced against the framework, admiring her in only underwear and bra. "You make a right pretty sight."

She whirled around, grabbed her dirty jeans off the floor, and threw them at him. "Get out if you're going to stand there and ogle me."

"Can't. Gotta get cleaned up and change too." Ambling into the room, he wrapped an arm around her naked waist and pulled her tight against him. Nuzzling her neck, then trailing kisses up her jawline to the corner of her mouth, he whispered against her lips, "One day, you'll not be able to resist me."

"Only when we are ready for eternity," she whispered, backsliding out of his grip and into the skirt and sweater. Next, she chose black boots and pulled them over her fresh socks. "I'm ready. Are you?"

"As soon as I shower. Can't stand this grit and soot." He disappeared into the bathroom. A few minutes later, he emerged, a towel wrapped low around his waist. "Like what you see?" He let the towel drop to the floor.

She coolly turned on her heel and murmured, "Angel, you're not. Tease and seducer you are. Shame on you."

He roared with laughter. "I'm a hot-blooded Scot warrior angel, not a goody-two-shoes. Nice to know I do affect you. I'll be out in a minute. We probably should leave Adventure here."

"Good idea. I'll leave food and water for her." Chinoah padded out to the living area where the dog curled up next to the cooling wood stove. She stirred up the embers and shoved in a few logs. Quickly flames raced up the wood. Brushing her hands together, she glanced at Addy. "We're going to go to the Holt Ranch for a while. You need to stay here. Guard the cabin."

The dog plastered its ears to its head and turned its back to her with a huff of displeasure.

"How about you join Killian and me next time I get to go for a run? You do know the landscape around here, right?" Silence greeted her question.

"Trying to bribe the dog?" he said in an amused voice.

"No, just reassuring her we are not abandoning her." She picked up her bag. "Ready."

Half-hour later, they arrived at the ranch. Caleb and Laurel greeted them at the stables. "What do you think of the horses?"

"Great riding horses. Are these the ones you want to sell?"

"I have several for sale, but these two will fit your needs. They are great in a saddle but don't mind pulling a carriage either." Caleb stroked the buckskin then offered a carrot. He did the same to the black horse.

"Speaking of carriage, how about we take a look before we settle down for dinner?" He moved forward to shake Caleb's hand in greeting.

"Want to get the business out of the way. Huh?" He took the reins and handed them to the waiting stable hands. Then paused. "Did you want to settle on the horses tonight?"

Killian glanced at Chinoah. "What do you think?"

"I liked the way my buckskin rode. She's single footed making for a smooth ride. What about yours?" Chinoah nodded in the direction of his slick black gelding.

"Powerful, but a smooth ride. If they won't balk at pulling a carriage I believe we have a deal." Killian patted the horse's neck.

"Great. I'll get the paperwork ready. Deliver it to you tomorrow along with the carriage, if you're interested."

Laurel blew out a breath. "These guys will talk horses and equipment forever. Come on in the house, and I'll show you around. Or would you rather walk with them?" A little boy came running across the field from the house. "When we gonna eat?"

"Soon, Jesse." She grabbed his hand. "Let's go wash up. Our friends will be joining us for supper."

The young boy turned his big eyes on Chinoah. She bent down and offered her hand. "Hi, Jesse, my name's Chinoah. Nice to meet you."

Jesse stood partly behind his mother's skirts. Slowly he reached out for her hand and gave it a quick shake.

"By all means, let's get washed up for supper. I'm kinda hungry too." She smiled at the young child, then switched her gaze to Laurel. "Lead the way. I'd love to see your ranch, but it's getting a bit dark. Maybe we can come back another time. I love that little stream that runs through your property."

Laurel's eyes went dreamy for a beat. "That's where Caleb and I met. It's a great picnic place." She picked up her skirts and led the way to the ranch house.

"We'll be right along. Won't take long to check out

the carriage." Caleb kissed his wife and motioned Killian to follow.

Once inside the barn, Caleb shoved open the large stall at the end of the barn. A skeleton of a carriage stood on four good wheels. "Here she is. Frame is in good shape. Got some rotting of the sideboards, the top needs some work, but otherwise, not bad."

Killian walked around the buggy, slid underneath it to check the springs and undercarriage. "I'll take it. A few hours of ironwork and new wood, she'll be great."

"There's a framework for a cloth bellows top. I believe Laurel was working on that. Not sure if she finished it or not, but it's close. Nice cover to keep the hot sun off while riding." Caleb glanced toward the ranch house. "Better get going. Laurel will have our heads if the meal gets cold."

"We'll pay her to finish the top."

"You'll have to take that up with her. Never meddle in Laurel's business. Not been married long but learned that right off. Happy wife, happy life." Caleb chuckled and strolled toward the house.

"Exactly." He kept pace with Caleb. "What do you want for the carriage?"

"Just getting it out of the barn is enough. Been sitting here for years. We talked about fixing it up, that's why Laurel was working on the top, but we're so busy with the ranch and her at the dress shop…"

"I won't let you just give it to me. Fair price?"

"How about we trade out farrier services? Shoe a couple of horses? I usually do my own, but I've a fence that needs repair. Believe some kids took an ax to it. If I catch 'em… Reported it to the sheriff, but he's got his hands full with the rowdy cowboys that came into town."

Caleb stopped and turned to him. "Heard you had a run-in with two of them."

"Chinoah had a run into a couple of cowboys this afternoon. She made short work of 'em. I arrived when it was nearly all over. Chinoah learned to take care of herself from an early age," he said proudly.

"Yeah, that's what Laurel said. Surprised the hell out of those men. I guess the other two rode through town shooting guns, scaring the horses and townsfolk. Widow Lowery grabbed the rifle from under the counter and rushed to the door. They were already gone." Caleb grinned. "Feisty old woman, but she's sure been good to Laurel and Jesse. Sheriff was none too happy having to chase them down. But he did, now they're all sharing a jail cell."

"Glad to hear it. I was a bit concerned riding out to your place with the other two still on the loose." Upon their return to the ranch house, Killian noticed both horses tied to the hitching post.

"If you have somewhere to keep the horses, you can ride them back to your cabin. If not, I'll hitch up the buckboard and give you and Chinoah a ride back." Caleb opened the screen and pushed open the door.

"We have an old barn. Not sure of its condition. But no feed and supplies for horses. I'll need to visit Wylder feed store tomorrow."

"Then we'll just use the buckboard tonight. Haul a few of Buttercup and Onyx's stuff to your barn. See what'll it take to fix it up. It was built before the cabin but never used. Heck, as you probably know, the landowner lost his ass in the California Gold mines and had to sell."

"Yeah, I've heard that story."

"Wash your hands," Laurel called. "Supper's ready."

Jesse climbed up in a chair and clapped his hands. "Hungry."

Caleb ruffled the boy's hair as he passed by. "We all are little man."

After washing their hands, the men sat at the table. Laurel said grace and passed the potatoes, gravy, and homemade wheat rolls. Caleb sliced the roast and sent the platter around the table.

"How are you liking Wylder?" Caleb stabbed his fork into a piece of roast and pointed it at Killian.

"Taking a little getting used to but seems like a right friendly town." He dished out potatoes on his and Chinoah's plate.

"Thanks, hon." Chinoah glanced at Caleb and Laurel. "Not had quite the problems we anticipated, which is good. I've a question for you, Laurel. In Scotland, I had split skirts for riding. Any chance you could make me a couple of pairs? Riding in a dress takes some finesse and I can't seem to master that—yet."

"Not sure what you mean, but if you draw me a picture, I'm sure I could create something you'd be happy with." Laurel scrunched up her face in concentration.

"I'll sketch for you before we leave tonight. Is that all right?" Chinoah slid a quick glance at Killian before returning her attention to Laurel.

Rest of the dinner conversation centered around the town, business owners, a bit of history of the Holt ranch, and the upcoming Harvest Ball.

Chapter Eleven

A Little Exercise and Pieces Parts for a Carriage

Under the shimmering light of the full moon, Chinoah and Killian waved from the cabin's porch to Laurel as they climbed in the back of the buckboard. Caleb clicked his tongue and snapped the reins. Buttercup and Onyx trotted off in the direction of the ranch.

"Caleb sure knows his horses," Killian remarked. "Those two will be perfect for us."

"True. We're going to have to add time to our schedule to prepare the horses for riding or hooking them up to the carriage. I didn't realize how in our time we simply pick up and go."

He rubbed his chin between thumb and forefinger. "Not exactly. Have to start the vehicle. Scrap off the ice or snow while you let the car warm up. It's just a different set of exercises. Life is slower here because it has to be."

"Guess you're right. But I don't have to like it," she huffed.

"Give it a chance. The pace may grow on you." He chuckled, tipped her head up, and kissed her. "In a couple of weeks, we'll angel power our way to Healing Waters. Spend a few days with Raymond and his wife. Should be a relaxing time."

"Shouldn't you be looking for the demon?"

"I've put feelers out. Raymond had the most information. Still, I would like to have talked to the leader of the rowdy cowboys. Strange, how he disappeared after the men got into trouble. Why, out of all the people in Jake's, two of them waited and attacked you."

"Maybe being Native American and a woman in pants was enough."

He shrugged. "Maybe. But my gut says no."

Caleb brought the buckboard to stop in front of the cabin. He turned in the seat. "See you all tomorrow."

Killian wrapped an arm around her waist and helped her out of the buckboard. "Yep. See you tomorrow."

Chinoah waved, then made her way to the cabin.

Arm still around her, he unlocked the door. "Shall we turn in? Got a busy day tomorrow with the orders we took today. Seems each day is busier than the day before."

"That's a good thing. Right?" She curled into him and rested her head on his shoulder. "No wind. Nice." Pausing, she glanced up at his strong jawline and high cheekbones. *My own Scottish Highlander. Seemed no matter what happened, the one corner of his mouth curved in a partial smile. Funny I'd never noticed that before.* "I've got the dress fitting tomorrow afternoon. Then the Harvest Ball is the next evening."

"Should have the carriage ready to take you to the ball. Cinderella." He hesitated and studied her. "You're not nervous, are you?"

"Of course not." She lied.

"It's late. But I'd like to check the barn. See if it's ready for a couple of horses, and their feed, hay, tack, and saddles. I'd like to store the carriage in there out of the weather too." He turned to her. "Up for a bit of a walk?"

"Sure. It's such a beautiful night compared to what we've experienced since we got here." She laced her fingers with his and whistled for the dog to follow. The closer they got, the better the barn looked. Of course, moonlight could camouflage problem areas. "Needs a coat of paint, but out here in the harsh weather, that's no surprise."

"Let's take a walk around the outside to make sure of its structural integrity. An owl hooted in the distance and coyotes yipped. The occasional light breeze rustled the bushes and dry grasses. The trees around the property cast eerie shadows under the full moon as they strolled around the structure. After looking the outside over, he pulled the double barn doors open.

Adventure scooted in ahead of them, sniffing in all the corners and running around. Using a bit of angel magic, he illuminated the interior. Four stalls with iron gates were on the left side. On the right was a huge area for storing tack, blankets, saddles, and three more stalls to the right.

Between the tack area and the first stall, a set of stairs led to the loft. "Stay," she commanded the dog, then wrinkled her nose as she and Killian climbed the stairs. "Smells like any hay in here is molded."

"I agree with you. Have to clean out up here." The loft appeared to be a flat surface from the top of the stairs spanning the back half of the barn, tall enough for him to stand. Several old bales of hay stacked in the back appeared molded. With a wave of his hand, the bales completely disappeared. "Can't have the horses coming in contact with the moldy hay should any fall through the floor or…" He put his arm across in front of her. "Stay here. Don't want you falling through any rotted wood planks."

He paused, stomped, and bounced on several of the floorboards. The wood planks *creaked* but held. "Seems solid enough." He grabbed hold of the railing across the front of the loft, tried to wiggle it, then attempted to shake the supporting wood pillars. "Well built structure." She joined him at the far end of the barn and carefully pushed open double doors. "Great view of the surrounding area. It looks like we have a few neighbors further out. Seen enough?"

"Yep. The barn's in fine shape to house the horses. Apparently, the previous owner planned on having several." He shrugged. "His loss is our gain."

After descending the stairs, he remarked, "The aisle between the sides is plenty wide enough to pull the carriage through and park it at the far end of the barn." He extinguished the light and shut the barn door.

"Good." She walked toward the cabin. When she opened the door and started inside, she paused and flipped around so quickly that Killian and the dog nearly ran right into her. "You promised Adventure and I a run tonight. Caleb is long gone by now. Besides, better chance we won't be seen this late. The full moon allows us natural light to avoid any animal traps."

Not waiting for his response, she stripped. Her form shimmered, blurred, and transformed into a sleek black wolf with startling amber eyes. Addy's tail wagged uncertainly as the dog approached the large wolf and sniffed. Satisfied, the pup whirled around and thundered out the door, across the porch, and down the steps before stopping to glance back and bark—an invitation to play.

"Guess I'm outvoted." He shed his coat and shirt, rolled his shoulders forward, and brought his marbled white and black wings forth. The tips extended to brush the floor before he spread them. With one strong bounce on the balls of his feet, he was airborne. The wolf howled and, with a strong leap, landed on the ground at the bottom of the cabin's steps. For the next hour, she and the dog raced around the property with Killian hovering six to ten feet above the ground, staying within sight of her in wolf form and the dog.

Finally, he motioned them all toward the cabin. "Enough fun for tonight." He held the door open, waiting for the canines.

Reluctantly, she trotted to the cabin. Adventure's tongue lolled out, panting hard. After several slurps of water, Addy curled up on the rug next to the fireplace. Chinoah shifted and padded over to the flames. Wrapping herself in the blanket from the back of the couch, she plopped down. The embers were still warm from this morning.

He tossed a couple of logs on the fire, then did the same to the wood stoves in the rooms they'd be using. "Feel better?" He eased down on the couch beside her and rubbed her shoulders.

"Much. But I'll be sore tomorrow. The ground is uneven. But thank you. Did you spot the two bear traps on the northwest boundary of our property line?"

"Yep. Those two are all I saw. And they're not on our property. So you've got a clean ten acres to run."

She stretched and yawned. "I'm ready for bed." Ambling into his bedroom, she showered, then slipped her nightgown over her head and sat on the edge of the bed.

"Me too. Are you sleeping with me tonight even though we're alone?"

"Got kinda used to your warm body next to mine." In truth, she was still shaken from the unprovoked encounter with the cowboys this afternoon. But there was no use telling him.

*Heaven knows he's protective enough over me.* She rolled into bed, pulling covers over her, fluffed her pillow, and heard him come out of the bathroom. The bed dipped as he climbed in beside her. His warm body and fresh spicy scent was the last thing she remembered drifting off to sleep.

****

Standing in front of the cabin door, Chinoah continued to tap her foot. Adventure trotted circles around her. "Hurry up, Killian. I need to get to the shop and do the bookkeeping this morning, so I can go over to have Laurel do the final fitting. The ball is tomorrow. I also want to pick up a little something for her from Wylder Side Bakery first."

Killian strolled out of the kitchen, straightening his coat, and pulling his gloves out of his pocket. "You've plenty of time. Settle down."

"Easy for you to say." She shot a scathing look in his direction.

"After today, we won't have to walk to the shop anymore. Either saddle up the horses or hook 'em up to the carriage."

"Either way, it beats going everywhere on foot. Don't mind the exercise but carrying packages to the cabin is tiring."

"True. Caleb should be at the shop this morning.

We'll ride over to Wylder Feed, get supplies for the horses. I hope they'll deliver out to the cabin."

She rushed back to the bedroom and picked a couple of everyday skirts, sweaters, and an apron or two out of the closet. Added a pair of ladies' shoes to the mix. "That should do it." Carefully, she folded them in the duffel, picked it up, and returned to the front door. She tossed the bag to Killian. "Would you mind carrying this for me? Figured after yesterday, I'd better dress the part away from the forge."

He caught the bag easily. "Sure. Not a bad idea. Not sure your clothing would have made any difference, but would have made it more difficult to fight the men off." Opening the door, he allowed the dog to race outside, followed by Chinoah. He closed the door and locked it.

At a brisk pace, they walked hand in hand to Dugan's. Adventure trotted beside her sniffing the air but never leaving her side.

The large cowbell above the door clanged their arrival. Luke turned and grinned. "Finally, beat you two here."

"Didn't know it was a contest." Killian chuckled. "You get employee of the month for going above and beyond."

"Chinoah, yesterday's receipts are in your desk drawer, and the cash is in the safe with the tally." Luke jerked his chin toward her office.

"I got the Wylders' wrought iron items done. Also, replacement railing for the Saloon. What do you want me to start on next?" Luke glanced at the tickets lined across the bench.

"Start on Roy's wagon repair. Caleb will be by shortly with a carriage that needs a few repairs. That's a rush job since I'll need it tomorrow night for the ball. Put the Holt ranch on your schedule for farrier services."

"Holt ranch. Ol' Joe been trying to get their business as long I've worked here. Caleb always said he did his own shoeing."

"May still be true, but we bartered a few things. The number of horses at the ranch has grown. Caleb's expanding doing a bit of select breeding of mustangs." Killian reached for his leather apron. Shook his head. "Who made your chaps and jacket?"

"After I burned my leg pretty bad the first couple weeks working for Joe, he sent me to Nartan at Sagebrush homestead. He paid for these custom chaps and jacket."

"Good of him," Killian commented. "Once I have transportation, I'll swing over to Sagebrush and talk to Nartan."

"I was off work for a few weeks after being burned. Said he couldn't afford for that to happen again. But that was just him hiding kindness."

"Gathering up the few completed tickets today." She dashed into her office and shut the door.

Three hours later, she emerged from her office dressed in a sky blue skirt, matching plaid blouse, and ladies' boots. She whirled a dark blue cape over her shoulders. Killian whistled. "Wow, looking good."

"Why, thank you, sir." She laughed and curtsied. "Decided to look presentable around town today. Might make it easier for the townspeople I haven't met to accept me at the ball tomorrow."

Luke turned a shy gaze on her. "You look mighty pretty Mrs. Dugan."

"Why, thank you, Luke. But it's still Chinoah,

whether I'm in jeans or a dress."

"Yes, ma'am, I mean Chinoah." Luke stammered.

"You and Jilly going to the ball tomorrow night?" She picked up the front of her dress and cape. "Don't want to take the blacksmith shop with me."

"Yes. Jilly made herself a dress. Really excited. Her mother and father are bringing meat and drink to the dance." Luke grinned.

"Oh." She scrunched her face up in a panic and turned to Killian. "Are we supposed to bring something too? Neither Cissy or Laurel mentioned it. Both knew we were planning to attend."

"Not sure. Didn't know anything about it." Killian scratched his chin, leaving black marks across his face, and his brow furrowed.

"Most everyone brings something to add to the refreshments." Luke waved his hand nonchalantly. "But you're new in town, so don't worry about it."

"I'm off to the dress shop. I'll ask Laurel what she thinks." She reached for the door handle. "No, Adventure. You need to stay this afternoon. I'll be back, and we'll have a good run at home." She knelt to scratch the dog's ears then winked up at her angel.

"Stay out of trouble." Killian strode over and kissed her.

"The trouble wasn't my fault." She motioned to her outfit then flipped her long, thick braid, tied with a light blue bow, over her shoulder. "Watch the dog. Let her out when necessary and go with her. Please."

"Yes, ma'am." He gave a sloppy salute.

Raising on tiptoe, she pressed her lips to his warmly as the bell sounded over the door. She jumped. Killian pulled her close out of Caleb's way as he entered the door.

"Did I interrupt something?" The ranch owner gave a hearty laugh.

"Nope," she said haughtily. "Was just leaving for the bank, dress shop, then a visit with Cissy. Not necessarily in that order." Blinking at the bright sunlight outside, she noticed Buttercup, Onyx, and two additional horses tied to the hitching post. Pieces of the carriage were stacked in the big wagon. One of Caleb's ranch hands stood beside the wagon. "Morning, Ma'am."

"Morning." She glanced back at Dugan's then up and down the street. "Gotta go. See you later." Before she left-turned the corner on Backstreet, she paused to look back to see the men lifting parts out of the wagon. She hustled up the street to Gold Mount Bank and made the deposit. After chatting for a couple of minutes, she said her goodbyes and continued her route to Wylder Street and the Wylder Side Bakery. She pushed the door open to the bakery. Delicious aromas of chocolate, a variety of cookies, and fresh-baked bread wafted around the room, making her mouth water. "Cissy, you here?"

The baker popped up from under the counter. "Of course. Where else would I be? Wow, don't you look nice."

"Decided I'd best to try to fit in around here when I'm away from the forge. I'll still be in jeans and sloppy shirts at the blacksmith shop. Costs too much in replacement clothes to wear anything else. Brought a few everyday skirts, blouses, and couple of dresses from the cabin to change into when I leave work."

"Most don't care what you wear. Those that do should mind their own business." She snickered. "Not that they ever will. Sure would have messed up those pretty clothes in the altercation yesterday. Buck claimed you wiped up the street with those cowboys. Where'd you learn to fight like that?"

"Survival when you are an Indian in a white man's world. The women talk behind your back. The men think they can take advantage of you. Only takes once for the men to learn. Then the women despise you for the respect earned. Can't win. Except for confident women like you and Laurel who aren't intimidated."

"You got that right. We aren't the only ones. What can I get for you?"

"I need a dozen cookies, different varieties for the women at the dress shop. I'm going for my final fitting this morning and picking up my ball gown."

"How exciting. I can't wait to see it tomorrow night. Caleb told Buck that Laurel finished the cover for the carriage. He's delivering it to Killian this morning. Heard you bought two Holt horses."

"Wow, news travels fast in this town. We just made those arrangements last night. We bought Buttercup and Onyx. Sweet horses. Killian thought he could get the carriage repaired enough to use it tomorrow to ride to the ball. I don't mind telling you I don't relish walking from the cabin to the hotel in my new ball gown."

Three more women came into the bakery. They glanced at Chinoah and whispered among themselves. "Good morning ladies. Have you met Chinoah Dugan? She's married to Killian Dugan, who bought the blacksmith shop. She does the bookkeeping for him." Cissy waved toward the woman.

"Chinoah, this is Pattie, Margaret, and Sally." Before she could finish introductions, another woman and a man strode into the bakery. "I better get back to work. See you tomorrow night." Cissy handed her a box of cookies tied with a red ribbon.

She took the box, paid Cissy, and nodded to the women. "Nice to meet you." Then turned her attention back to Cissy. "See you at the ball." She strolled out of the bakery and down Sidewinder Lane with her box of cookies. The bell chimed as she entered Lowery's Dress Shoppe. "I've got treats," she announced.

Mrs., Lowery looked up from her desk at the end of the counter. For a moment, her eyebrows raised. "Here for your last fitting?"

"Yes. I'm so excited." She presented the box of cookies. "Take a couple. I'll take the rest to Laurel, Leona, and the others upstairs."

Widow Lowery peered in the box and gingerly took two, then nodded upstairs. "She's waiting for you. Don't get crumbs on the dresses." Then she took a bite of cookie and went back to shuffling paperwork.

Chinoah raced up the steps and was greeted by a smiling Laurel holding the finished gown, in light rust with scalloped neckline, fitted bodice, and full-length skirt, also with scalloped edges. "You look nice. Come try it on."

She sucked in a breath, handed the cookie box over to Laurel, and hesitantly brushed her fingers on the soft silky material. "It's absolutely beautiful," she said in an awed voice.

Laurel took the box and inhaled. "You've been to Cissy's. Thank you so much." Then led the way behind the partitions. "I wasn't sure what shoes you'd be wearing, so added just a little length to allow for heels."

"Very low heels. Almost exactly like these." She glanced down at her shoes.

"Perfect." Laurel shooed her behind the dressing dividers.

She took the dress and stepped behind the partition. The dress slipped over her like butter and hugged her curves, but not too tightly. It was quite comfortable. Whirling around once, she nearly knocked down the divider. Then she sashayed into the seamstress room.

Quiet ooh's and ahh's filled the room. "It's gorgeous," another seamstress whispered, then motioned for her to spin around. "Look at that flow." This woman had been a little stand-offish, but now she gushed over the dress. *Maybe I can fit in here without repercussions after all.*

Standing on tiptoe, she spun around again. The dress cleared the floor an inch or so which was perfect. She paused. "Can I ask you a question?"

"Of course." Laurel glanced expectantly at her.

"The ball. Is everyone expected to bring some type of refreshment?" She shifted from barefoot to barefoot.

Laurel giggled. "Heard about that, huh? Yes, the good cooks and bakers bring food to share at the ball. Others bring drink. But since you are new, the sign-up list wouldn't have reached you. However, you can bet they will for the Christmas Ball."

"Okay. So should I at least bring drinks? I haven't gotten the hang of cooking or baking on the stove in the cabin." She snapped her fingers. "Can I go ahead and commission a dress just like this only in a sparkly bright green material? I love the feel and movement of this gown."

"Sure. I can start searching for the material right away. Now go take off the dress so I can box it up for you." Laurel watched her flounce across the floor on her tiptoes to the partition.

"I'll write up the receipt, and you can take it down to Mildred." Laurel pulled out a sheet of paper.

"Excellent. I brought money to pay for it today." She slipped the dress over her head and pulled on her skirt and blouse. Tugged on socks and shoes, then she waltzed out from behind the divider and handed the dress to Laurel. "I'll just run down and pay for this while you box it up."

She handed the receipt and the money to widow Lowery. Footsteps sounded on the stairs as Laurel brought down the dress in a box.

"Hey, have you thought any more about the split riding skirt we discussed?" She took the box from the seamstress.

"I have. Working on a design and material that will take the wear and tear you'll put it through. Let you know when I've got it finished."

"Thanks!" She waved and walked out of the shop smiling wide. *A successful trip with no problems.*

Chapter Twelve

A Carriage Fit for a Queen and Harvest Ball Escapade

Killian, Caleb, Luke, and Cane brought the carriage parts into the shop. Then Caleb and Cane made one more trip to the wagon and brought in the finished cloth bellows top. "It took Laurel an hour to finish it last night." Caleb held it up proudly. "Great work."

"How much? I'm happy to pay her."

"Want to make sure it fits and is what you want. Then we'll talk price. She initially made it for us, but I bought her a new buggy. No time or tools to make repairs. I'm glad you could use the old one. When do you want me to bring my horses by for shoeing?"

"Either Luke or I can be out at your ranch day after tomorrow mid-morning."

"Works for me. How about we take a ride over to the feed store? I can load the supplies in my wagon and drop them in your barn on the way back to the ranch." Caleb slapped his hat against his leg and put it back on his head.

"Stopped by the barn on the way in. Looks great. The horses should be happy. I noticed a couple of loose boards and a broken one in your corral attached to the barn. Might want to repair those before you let either horse out there on their own. Buttercup is an escape artist."

"Sounds great. I'll take care of the repairs tonight." He turned to Luke. "Can you hold the fort down until I get back? Keep an eye on Adventure. The dog gets into trouble and we'll both be in the dog house."

"Sure. Dog's never been a problem. Plenty of work on this carriage, or do you want me to work on the orders due out tomorrow?" Luke held up several orders.

"Finish what you're doing on the carriage and then start on the orders. I can stay late to finish the carriage for tomorrow night. Chinoah and I will ride Buttercup and Onyx to the cabin tonight. She'll appreciate the ride." He opened the door for Caleb and Cane, then followed them out.

Caleb tipped his hat back on his head. "Sounds like there's not enough of you to go around. How about I leave Cane at the cabin to do the repairs?" He turned to his ranch hand. "Got anything that can't wait at the ranch?"

"Not that I think of boss." Cane answered, climbing into the wagon.

"Good." Caleb switched his attention back to Killian. "Won't take him long, provided you have the wood. Then we'll barter out more horseshoeing for his labor."

"You don't have to do that. But I'd appreciate the help. You're right. I'm spread pretty thin right now. The incomplete orders that Joe left are killing us. Should even out soon. Or I'll need to add another apprentice." He paused to scratch his head.

"I believe there is a stack of lumber in the front right side of the barn." He untied Onyx's reins and eased on to his back. Buttercup snorted her displeasure, pawing the ground and plastering her ears to her head at being left behind.

Caleb hooted with laughter. "Yeah, she's got a bit of an attitude about being left. She'll get over it, especially if you have an apple or carrot around."

When Killian returned, Luke had the majority of the welding done on the undercarriage. The cloth top was in place. He wasn't sure about the ruffled edges around the front, but Chinoah would love it. "You been busy, Luke. What you got left?"

"Couple spokes in the wheels need to be replaced. Not sure how you'll match the red the others are painted. I forged a few replacement parts. They're over on the table."

"Thanks, I'll take it from here. You go ahead and get on the work due tomorrow." He rubbed the back of his neck and shoulder. *This manual labor was more difficult than I imagined. I'll give Nat an ear full when I return. Battling demons is one thing. Pounding out iron and steel with primitive means was another.*

By the time Chinoah returned from her errands, it was time to close up shop. When she entered, Adventure raced to the door, all wiggles and wagging tail. Bending down, she gave the dog's ears a good rub before picking up the receipts off the counter. Taking cash from the register into her office, she put it in the safe. After Killian sauntered in and closed the door, she wiped a black smudge off his cheek and kissed him. She lingered and savored every moment as she leaned into him.

His hands slid around her waist. He held her tight against him enjoyed the feeling of his woman wrapped around him. *I'll never let you go. I just need to find a way to convince you I'm in this relationship for the long haul.*

Desire bubbled up inside him like a fiery volcano. He went hard and slipped his hands down to cup her arse, pressing his arousal against her.

Then his hand trailed up, pulled her blouse out of her skirt, and fingers eased inside her bra to caress her firm, voluptuous breast. He could sense she was as aroused as he. Visions danced in his brain of picking her up, scooting her on the counter, lifting her skirts, and spreading those long legs. *This was not helping.* Despite taking several deep breaths in an attempt to calm the beast inside, his desire ran rampant.

Raising his mouth from hers, he gazed at her closed eyes, wondering what was going on behind them. *How long can I keep my physical and emotional needs bottled up inside? I'm a warrior angel, not a damn saint. This assignment couldn't have come at a worse time. I had it all worked out when we left for Scotland. Damn Commander North.*

Suddenly her dark chocolate eyes blinked open and gazed into his. "Eternity is getting closer and closer." Her fingers threaded through the baby fine hair at the nape of his neck. She made no move to put distance between them. A door slammed, and footsteps echoed in the forge. *Shit. Luke was still here.*

She quickly backed away, straightening and tucking her blouse. "I'll deal with these receipts tomorrow." She opened the door. "What'd you do to Buttercup? She's not happy with you."

"Okay, if I leave now?" A red-faced Luke hurried toward the door. "Meeting Jilly at her parents' place for dinner and game night."

"Sure Luke. And thanks. See you tomorrow." He swiveled his head to Chinoah. "Attitude stems from having to stay here while Onyx and I went to the feed store with Caleb." He went on to tell her about the repairs needed on the corral. Caleb's offer and the rest of his day until Luke closed the door and his footfalls disappeared outside.

"If not for Luke, I would have put you up on this counter, pulled up your skirts, spread your legs, bared your womanly parts to me, and had my way with you." He growled seductively, changing his stance in an effort to relieve the tightening in his crotch.

Panting slightly, Chinoah pursed her lips. "And I probably would have let you. Consequences be damned. But Luke was here, and we've come to our senses."

"Speak for yourself, woman." Sending caution to the wind, he grabbed her around the waist, lifted her onto the counter, yanked up her skirts, and shoved between her spread legs. His fingers quickly found the crotch of her moist panties, teased them aside, and caressed her soft folds.

She squealed, then slapped her hand over her mouth and twisted to peer at the door. "It's unlocked."

"And you're wet." He thrust a finger inside and curled it into her sweet spot while his thumb rubbed the tender bundle of nerves.

"Oh—God—Killian." She grabbed his shoulders and writhed against his ministrations as wave after wave of ecstasy shot through her. Finally pliant, she eased back.

"Wow, it's a while for you too, or I'm one hell of a lover."

"Don't go getting a big head about it," she panted.

"Too late, already built to please a woman." He snickered and brushed his lips over hers, then trailed kisses to her cleavage, his tongue licking inside her blouse while he unbuttoned it.

"Mighty cocky, aren't you?" She slapped a hand over her mouth.

Pausing to glance up at her, one corner of his mouth quirked up, and he raised an eyebrow. "Oh, just full of double entendres, aren't you? But you'd be right. I have the right equipment." With a flick of his fingers, her bra released and spilled her breasts into his awaiting hands. Sucking each nipple until they were hard berries, he let his hand wander lower until he could caress her center. "Shall we?"

She pushed at him. Jerked up and attempted to button her blouse. "Shall we what? You're still fully dressed. The door is unlocked. Anyone could walk in." Still, she reached up, unbuttoning his shirt.

"Send mixed messages much?" He grinned wickedly as his fingers danced and teased her center. "If I weren't dressed, without thought or intent, we'd be facing eternity together. Married under angel law. I wouldn't have been able to stop myself. As it is, it's still a close call." He bent his head and sucked on her breasts as his arousal grew and begged for release. "Besides, a little risk adds to the experience, don't you think?"

She pulled her blouse together, pushed him aside, and jumped off the counter. Stomping to the door, she yanked the shade down and locked the door. Stalking back to him, without warning, she flicked open the button on his jeans, tugged his pants and boxers down to his ankles. While he was off-balance, she toppled him into a chair and knelt down between his spread legs. "Let's see if the experience is still stimulating without the risk." She pleasured him for only a few minutes before he moaned deeply and bucked his release.

"Hmmm. Still stimulating. Now, what were you saying about a long time?" She slapped his naked hip and stood. "Don't you ever put me in such a position again. Don't you understand these people look at me differently? If someone had walked in, it would have been understood why you took a squaw as your wife. She'll do anything, anywhere. Whereas you, they'd applaud your sexual prowess. At least the men would. The women—" She tapped her finger to her lips and glanced coyly at him from under her long, dark eyelashes. "—might be jealous."

"Sorry. I didn't think of that." He stood and dressed, leaving his shirt unbuttoned and a mischievous glint in his eye. A brow raised, he snatched her around the waist and plopped her back on the counter, wedging himself between her legs. "As long as we are experimenting, let's check your hypotheses."

She squealed. "Let me go."

"Now you don't mean that, darl'n," his Scottish brogue thick. "I'm an angel and a male. I know these things." Hungrily, he took her mouth with his while leaning her back and lifted her skirts, slipping his fingers underneath her panties again. As he suspected, she was still wet and ready. Slower this time, his fingers feathered, teased, touched, and caressed her intimate parts as she undulated beneath him. He spread her legs, moved the crotch of her panties aside, and slid lower down her body easing her legs over his shoulders.

Her eyes wide, she gulped in air. "What are you doing?" When he gently blew a warm breath across her bared folds, she moaned and spread wider. He considered burying himself inside her, but according to angel law, that would constitute taking her as his wife without her consent. An offense severely punished by the Angel Tribunal. Nope, this loophole of pleasure would have to suffice until… The tip of his tongue teased her opening and the sensitive little bundle of nerves.

Moaning his name, she fisted her fingers in his hair. He thrust one long finger then two inside her, and the hot tide of passion raged through her like a molten river of lava as he continued to draw out her pleasure. At last, the pulsing subsided. Spent, she relaxed against him. "Yep. You're right. Still stimulating. Maybe even more so without the risk factor of being caught." He snickered and raised to kiss her.

She returned his kiss with reckless abandon, then whispered against his lips. "I love it when I'm right."

"Unless you want to test this further, we might want to get dressed and head to the cabin. Then, if you are still interested, we can explore tempting eternity." He lifted her off the counter, letting her warm curvy body slide against his, then lowered her to her feet. The skirt caught in his hand, his fingers brushed between her legs, and then he let the garment fall. "A reminder of what you're missing."

She shivered and slapped at him. "Got it."

They dressed. He finished closing up and met her at the door in coat, hat, and gloves. "Ready to go?"

Already in her coat, she wrapped the scarf around her neck, pulled on her hat, whistled for Adventure, and stepped out the door. "More than ready. I felt like I've hiked twenty miles today before I got here, and we…" She carefully put her dress box partially in the saddlebag, put her foot in the stirrup, and slung her leg over the horse. Astride the horse, she changed her mind and arranged the box in front of her. "Wait until you see the dress. Laurel is also working on a split skirt for riding and a Christmas Ball gown like the Harvest one, only in a shimmering bright kelly green material. If she can find it. Otherwise, something close. Killian, would you let Addy ride with you? I don't have room."

"Of course." He scooped the dog up. "The dress sounds terrific. Are you modeling the dress tonight?" A seductive smiled curved his lips.

"Of course. But it's not an invitation for a repeat performance."

"Aww, you spoil all my fun." His lower lip formed a pout.

"I beg to differ with you. For an angel, you are sure a pain when it comes to…" She trailed off. "Still, you are male. I guess it's to be expected."

"Didn't hear any complaints a little while ago. Still, I'm glad you noticed. Now let's take advantage of it." He waggled his eyebrows and urged his horse into a trot toward the cabin.

She raised a brow and brought her horse up beside his. "There's this little issue of eternity." Pausing, she changed the subject. "I must say this is so much faster than walking. Will the carriage be ready for tomorrow night?"

"You bet." *It will be ready even if I have to use a little angel magic.* "You won't be walking to the ball in your new gown, Cinderella. He snickered under his breath.

****

The next day dawned in bright sunshine. The hours flew by as they worked at the forge. He closed early, as did several businesses in town, allowing everyone time

135

to get ready for the Harvest Ball.

"Sorry, Addy, you have to stay tonight. Be a good girl, and we'll go for a run tomorrow night." She scratched the dog under the chin and peered into her eyes. "I promise."

The dog thumped her tail twice. Circled on her blanket and plopped down in front of the wood stove in the living area, emitting a low disgruntled huff.

Butterflies flitted in Chinoah's belly as she climbed into the refurbished carriage with bright red wheels, black metal gloss trim, and burnished wood frame. The leather top with red trim scallops Laurel had created matched perfectly. She arranged her rust-colored gown, flipped her long braid woven with fall flowers over her shoulder, and glanced at Killian. He stood watching with male appreciation.

"You are absolutely beautiful." He took her hand and kissed it. "Just like Cinderella." Hopping in, he wrapped a blanket around her, eased down beside her, and took the reins. "Sun goes down in these parts, and it gets cold. Even though it was a beautiful day."

"You look quite handsome in your western suit and tie. Didn't know you owned one."

"There a lot of things you don't know about me. But I'm sure you'll discover since we are living under the same roof." A deep chuckle rose from his throat.

"And working in the same place." Her eyes sparkled as she glanced at the star-strewn sky. "No clouds to keep the heat in. At least there is no wind. So we better not complain."

Her innuendo to their activities last evening wasn't lost on him. She stirred his blood like no other. "You got that right." He leaned over and kissed her cheek.

Something had changed between them since yesterday. She was more relaxed and responded to his teasing with amused ease and a less sharp tongue.

Perhaps he'd been oblivious to the toll this assignment and life in 1878 had taken on her. *She's a mortal native American woman/shifter, not a battle-ready warrior. I need to pay more attention to her.* He clicked his tongue and gave the reins a snap. Buttercup and Onyx trotted toward town, and he rested his arm around her shoulders.

The hotel was decorated in fall foliage, pumpkins, and haystacks. A large scarecrow lounged against the door frame. Festive lanterns lit the front entrance. He pulled back on the reins and jumped out, tying them to the hitching posts. He walked to her side and offered his hand. "M'lady."

She started to take his hand. He put his hands around her waist and lifted her effortlessly out of the carriage.

Sucking in a breath, she leaned in and kissed him. "Thank you, kind sir," she said against his lips.

"Hey Killian, you're going to give the rest of us a bad rep with our ladies if you continue with the white knight stuff." Caleb clapped him on the shoulder and glanced at Chinoah. "Wow! What a stunning gown. Laurel made that," he said proudly.

"She did a wonderful job." Chinoah touched the dress and moved to make it swirl.

"Since when do you notice a woman's dress?" Killian joked.

"Since I'm married to a seamstress and a damn good one." Caleb grinned as Laurel came up behind him.

"Oh, stop. Caleb. It's mighty cold out here. Why don't we go on into the ballroom?" Laurel slipped her hand through the crook of Caleb's arm, glided up the steps, and into the hotel.

"He's not wrong," Chinoah sashayed into the hotel, causing her dress to swirl around her. "Lead the way."

Inside the ballroom, it appeared the whole town had turned out for the gathering. Men and women decked out in their Sunday best chatted in small groups. A few gave her a cold stare, especially the cronies sitting with Mrs. Chambers. Chinoah made a point of stopping by their table, introducing herself and exchanging greetings.

Though Mrs. Chambers never said a word, the others in her group were more gracious. Most of the townsfolk came over, introduced themselves, and made them both feel welcome. Several long tables were assembled along one wall with food and drink. A group of musicians gathered in the far corner, tuning up their instruments, then began playing a variety of songs.

"Care to dance, m'lady?" He swept down in a bow, took her hand, and kissed it.

"Of course." Holding the sides of her soft dress, she curtsied.

He gathered her into his arms and glided her around the dance floor. She melted against him, resting her cheek on his chest. He kissed the top of her head and let the music take them away. Too soon, the music stopped, and an upbeat tempo replaced the dreamy romantic notes.

"Want something to eat?" He glanced toward the tables, lacing his fingers with hers.

"Yes." She followed him through the crowd, stopping to talk with Luke and Jilly, snuggled together at a corner table, visited with other people she knew and townsfolk who introduced themselves. Gathering food on their plates, they settled at a table at the edge of the room beside Cissy and Buck. Laurel and Caleb joined them a few minutes later.

It seemed everyone had heard about the new blacksmith and his wife. By the end of the night, they'd danced nearly every dance except while they visited with friends and enjoyed the great food.

"My feet won't take much more in these shoes. I doubt the townspeople would appreciate me taking them off."

"No, probably not. Or the idea would catch on, and all the women would be running around barefoot, and it would be your fault. A no-win situation for you," he teased.

They said their goodbyes and walked toward the door. Two cowboys swaggered into the ballroom, talking loudly and laughing. Killian stiffened and stepped in front of Chinoah. "You boys lost?" The magic rolled off one of the troublemakers from a few days ago, called boss. Quickly the magic signature disappeared, then wavered in and out. Killian raised a brow.

*The man was too drunk to keep his disguising spell in place.* "The saloon is down the street and around the corner." The angel pointed to the door. *I don't want to get into a tussle with this magic wielder, no telling what he might do. The last thing I need to happen is to be outed in public. Or maybe he's faking it.*

He glanced around the ballroom. Only a few seemed to notice the situation. Caleb, Luke, and a couple of men he didn't know were slowly walking toward him. Hoping there were no unknown magic beings here, he grasped the cowboy's arm and pushed angel influence on him. "Time to go."

Confused, the man shook his head and glared at Killian. "We just got here. Going to have a good time."

"You'd enjoy yourselves more at the Wylder County Social Club across the railroad tracks." The angel waggled his brows. "Know what I mean?"

The man leered at Chinoah. "Lots of pretty women here."

"Believe me. They're trouble to you two. Best if you seek fun elsewhere." Killian increased the magic as Buck, Caleb, Luke, and two other men surrounded the group.

The boss nodded. "You may be right. Come on." Boss motioned for the man that came in with him to follow, then staggered toward the door. Killian followed them and watched as the men stumbled down the hallway and outside.

He breathed a sigh of relief, still unsure if it was an act. The old grandfather clock standing in the lobby chimed the hour of eleven-thirty. The townspeople gathered their empty dishes left on the tables and headed for the exits. The musicians had packed up earlier. Most waved goodbye. He decided it was a good time for them to leave.

As luck would have it, Caleb and Laurel, Buck and Cissy were ready to leave at the same time. *Safety in numbers.* They walked out as a group. The women were chatting, and the men hesitating only a moment to look up and down the deserted street.

He turned to Caleb. "Either Luke or I will be out first of the week to shoe your horses. After that, got business up north mid-week, so Chinoah and I will be gone for a few days. Luke will be holding down the fort."

"Next week then." Caleb helped Laurel into their

buggy and then waved.

Killian swung Chinoah into their carriage. As he snapped the reins, lightning streaked across the sky, ending in a ball of power out toward their cabin. A loud boom shook the ground.

"Great, we'll get rain, then snow," Buck complained, helping Cissy into their buckboard tied beside Killian's. "Weather's crazy this year."

Killian made a noncommittal sound, raised one hand in a wave, then slapped the reins to quicken the horses' pace.

Chapter Thirteen

Unexplained Magic, a Cozy Weekend, and a Run of Trouble

Killian and Chinoah arrived home, where nothing appeared to be disturbed. Yet they both felt and smelled the magic around the cabin, but the trail faded out across the meadow. No signs of horses or a wagon.

The weekend was uneventful. The sun warm, the wind calm enough to go for a couple of rides around the property. Onyx and Buttercup enjoyed their much-needed exercise. A pretty stream babbled through the far end of the property, where rocks jutted out of the ground making a small waterfall. Curled up on the couch with her head on his shoulder, they shared popcorn and wine. The altercation at the ball faded away.

After a restless Sunday night, Chinoah got up before the sun, took the dog outside, and paused. Surveying the surrounding area, she sniffed, undressed, leaving her clothes folded neatly on the porch chair. "Come girl, lets you and I go for a run." As if a trick of light, she shimmered into a sleek black wolf and padded down the steps with Adventure close on her heels.

On all fours, she raced across their land. The never-ending wind rustled the blades of grass and twigs on the bushes, whistling around the barn and cabin. The scent of wildlife on the breeze, sleepy bird songs, and wing flaps of feathered predators racing toward their prey were much more stimulating in wolf form.

Scenting wild rabbits, she gave chase until the trail ended at a small stream that flowed through their property. She splashed through the water, crossing to the other side. Picking up the scent of antelope, she followed that for a while. Free to run and explore was exhilarating.

Approximately an hour later, she and the dog returned to the cabin. As the sun peeked over the horizon spreading bright yellow rays across the dusky sky, she shifted back to human. On the porch, she snatched her clothes and pushed open the cabin door. Still breathing hard, she quickly dressed and walked into the kitchen, the panting dog trotted beside her, and she froze.

Killian sat at the kitchen table, sipping his coffee. A half-empty plate of eggs, toast, and possibly bacon sat in front of him. A steaming mug of hot cocoa sat next to a plate of scrambled eggs and bacon. His face blank, he stared at her with those penetrating blue eyes set in a beautifully sculpted face showing signs of controlled fury. "You know this is 1878. They shoot wolves on sight because they are considered a problem for the ranchers. There is a high bounty on wolves for their pelts. A shiny black one would bring a great price."

She met his gaze. Even angry, he was spectacularly handsome. "I, uh, didn't think of that," she stammered.

His nostrils flared as his eyes narrowed. "Obviously. You didn't think. Period. We agreed you'd run only with me and after dark. Not because I want to control you but because I want to protect you."

"I couldn't sleep. It was dark when I left. The sun is just now peeking over the horizon. I took Adventure with me," she argued.

"So she could come back alone after you'd been killed. Or perhaps get her killed too?" Unbridled fury flashed in his eyes as he shoved the plate of half-eaten food to the center of the table, downed the rest of his coffee, and pushed up from the table. "Eat, and we'll be off." He stalked into the bathroom and closed the door harder than necessary.

Famished, she gobbled down the food on the plate and drank the hot chocolate. Sitting at the kitchen table, she watched out the window as the sun rose and spread an orange glow over the land, then got to her feet. *He was right. Geeze—I hate when he's right. What a stupid thing to do. I endangered my life, Adventure's life, and the assignment. Though he hadn't mentioned that yet.*

Washing the dishes, she put them away, slipped on her coat, hat, gloves, and wound the scarf around her neck. She hesitated, then tucked a carrot and apple in her pocket and walked out to the barn to find both horses saddled. *He must have gotten up right after I left.*

At the gate to their stalls, she paused to offer a carrot to Buttercup, who neighed softly and nudged her with her nose. Onyx snatched the apple, snorted, and pawed the ground, anxious to be on his way.

Boots crunched on the gravel as Killian strode into the barn. "Ready to go?" His voice still held a bit of irritation but not nearly as furious as when he left the house.

"I'm sorry. It won't happen again. I got too wound up at the ball with the altercation. I couldn't settle down. A run always puts things right." She mounted Buttercup and waited for Killian to say something. He swung into the saddle, clicked his tongue, allowing Onyx to set the pace to Dugan's.

"We're leaving at noon for Healing Waters. Adventure will accompany us. Not sure if our cover was blown Friday night or not. But it's time to take the offensive. I don't want to wait until midweek. Need to capture the demon and send him back where he belongs. Or at the very least get a bead on where he is hanging out and what he is planning." He paused, studying her. The leather in his saddle creaked as he turned, pointing a finger at her. "You'll stay in human form until such time as I deem it safe. Understood?"

His tone and authoritative attitude rankled, but she remained silent. Best to choose her battles. This wasn't one she'd win. She urged her horse into a canter, then full gallop, until she saw Adventure trying to keep up with her and Buttercup. Killian was hanging back for the dog. It was going to be one of those days.

Reining the horse in, she called Addy to her, took one foot out of the stirrup, leaned over snatching the dog off the ground and securing Adventure in front of her. The dog's tongue was hanging out. The poor thing was panting hard.

"Sorry. Again I didn't think. Settle down. You'll ride up here the rest of the way." When Killian rode by her, she swore he had a slight smile curving his full lips. *Damn him.*

Already dismounted, Killian tied Onyx to the hitching post in front of Dugan's Blacksmith and took Adventure from her. She swung her leg over and jumped to the ground. The dog barked as if happy to be on her own four paws and ran to the shop door.

He unlocked the door, held it open for Chinoah. After Addy barreled through, he stepped inside. "Luke." Pausing, he glanced around, lit the forge and lamps.

145

Picked up wood and stoked the woodstove near her office.

She went into the office, lit her lamp, and found the pile of receipts from yesterday. The dog curled up on the rug beside her desk.

"Luke?" He called up the stairs. "Guess he's not here yet. I hope…"

Noting the worry in his voice, she came out of the office. "Do you think something happened to Luke?"

"It's not like him to be late."

"He's not late." She sighed. "We're early. Because I…"

"Let not go into that again. Water under the bridge as long as you stick to the plan." A line dug itself between his eyebrows as his forehead creased. "After last night… Maybe I should…"

"You know, he could have spent the night with Jilly," she suggested. "They were getting awfully cozy at the dance after a couple of beers. I think Jilly had wine."

A devilish smile curved his lips. "Think so?"

She raised an eyebrow. "I do. So we are leaving this afternoon? I didn't pack."

"Not a problem. We need to leave from the cabin anyway."

With a bit of trepidation, she wondered what they would find in Healing Waters. After last night, she was pretty sure the demon had discovered their presence. *But what is in Wylder that would attract a demon from the present? Why the magic residue around their cabin, yet nothing was disturbed?*

The door to the building banged open, wind swept through the room, taking the day's orders, and swirling them to the ground. Luke stood in the doorway looking like the cat that ate the canary. "Wow, you two are early." The blush began at the base of his neck and continued to the tip of his ears and forehead.

"You're later than usual." Killian stared at the young man for a minute and burst out laughing. "Guess you're right, Chinoah."

"Of course. Expect nothing less when it comes to love or …" She giggled.

"Okay, so what is the joke at my expense?" Luke glared from Killian to her.

"Oh, Killian was worried that the altercation from Friday night had somehow spilled over to you. I figured it was an altercation of a pleasurable kind." She polished her nails on her sweater. "Appears I was right."

"I don't know what you two are talking about." Luke turned on his heel and marched to the forge, picked up a stock of metal with tongs, stuck it in the coals, and ignored them both. The metal heated up to a glowing red. He swung a hammer and beat the heck out of it.

This time she laughed out loud. "Kid, you gotta practice a poker face. The blush over your entire neck and face tells it all." She returned to the office and pulled out the ledgers. Pulling the money out of the safe, she completed the paperwork for the deposit then reconsidered. Not enough to require a trip to the bank now that the wind was whipping again. Perhaps leaving seed money for the next couple of days while they were gone was a good idea.

"Hey, Killian." She stepped out of the office. Luke was pounding the piece of metal harder and longer than she'd seen him do before. To be heard, she walked out on the main floor and tapped Killian on the shoulder. He turned, a broad grin on his face. She motioned him into her office and relayed her thoughts.

"Sounds like a plan. I'll let Luke know as soon as he's done beating the shit out of that piece of metal. Guess we shouldn't have teased him about Jilly."

"Probably. I've never seen a young man so naive to the ways of the world." She shook her head.

"From what I gather, his parents were Quaker. He broke from them and is trying to find his own way. He and Jilly have dated for about a year. From what I hear, the relationship is serious. Her parents like him."

"Wow, look at you gathering all the town gossip." She sighed and closed the ledger books. "I'm done for the day, unless you want me to go to the bank."

"Not necessary. Not gossip. I asked him point-blank and apologized for the ribbing. Not my place as his boss."

"True. So why's he hell-bent on decimating that piece of metal?"

Killian shrugged. "Don't know. Not going to ask either." He returned to the forging area, leaving the office door open, and touched Luke on the shoulder.

His apprentice stopped mid-strike and turned to him, then looked down at the floor. "It shouldn't have happened. Not yet."

She peeked around the doorway to the room and saw the light dawning for Killian. Quickly, she ducked further into the office before Luke could see her but continued to listen and peek once in a while.

"We are going to be gone for a couple of days. Leaving sooner than anticipated, something came up." He paused, looking at Luke's miserable face. "Do you want to talk about it?"

"No. Yes. Maybe." Luke slammed the hammer

down, tossed the metal in the bin, and looked toward the office warily. "It was our first time. We ain't married or even engaged. It wasn't planned. Just happened."

"I see. Did you take precautions?"

"Yeah. But. It's the principal. I didn't—we didn't mean. You know what I mean?" He looked at his boots and shifted from foot to foot, kicking at a piece of gravel on the wood floor. "Afterward, she was so soft and warm in my arms. We fell asleep together. When I woke, the sun was up, and I was late. I rushed out of the house without a word. I didn't know what to say."

Killian's lips twitched as he rubbed his chin. "The thing is, if you both enjoyed it, took precautions, and you plan a future together, it's inevitable. Or at least in most cases. The way I see it is you can't undo the act, but if you both feel you need to wait, then that's what you do from now on. Don't let misplaced guilt ruin what's between you. Leaving without a word was bad.

"If she's like most women, and lord knows I don't profess to be an expert on women, she'll be hurt. Discuss the act with her, decide on a course of action going forward, and that's it. Another thought, you might want to keep this situation between you and Jilly. Well, now I know, but it won't go any farther." He ran his fingers through his hair. "Chinoah and I have to go. You going to be all right?"

Luke puffed out his cheeks and blew out a breath. "Yes. I'll talk with Jilly tonight. Thanks for the advice. Women are such a tangle."

"And that will never change. One more thing. Could you take care of the horses while we're gone? There is plenty of feed and hay in the barn. You're free to stay at our cabin in the guest room until we get back. If you run into a problem, give Caleb a shout."

"Sure thing, boss." Luke grinned from ear to ear.

She bit the side of her cheek to keep from laughing at both men's discomfort. It seemed discussing touchy-feely things was difficult even for an angel. Still, she exited the office. "We ready?"

"Yes," Killian said firmly.

"Oh, Luke, if you get a lot of cash, I've left deposit slips in my desk drawer. Just take the money to the bank. Otherwise, put it in the safe. I'll take care of it when we get back." She put her hand on his arm. "Everything will be fine. You'll see." She nodded at the door where Jilly had quietly slipped inside.

"Morning Jilly," she said cheerfully. 'Now you keep this man in line while we're gone." She waved a hand in Luke's direction.

Red patches bloomed on Jilly's cheeks. "That's a tall order, ma'am."

"It's Chinoah. I've a feeling you're up to the task."

Killian slung his arm around her shoulder and kissed her affectionately. She wrapped her arm around his waist and squeezed. After putting on their outerwear, they stepped out and whistled for Adventure. The dog trotted out the door. He closed it leaving Luke and Jilly to sort out their problems.

"Whew, I hate handing out advice on matters of the heart. Never know when it's going to blow up in your face." He took his hat off, brushed a hand over his forehead, then replaced the cowboy hat.

"You did good." She kissed his nose, then brushed her lips over his. Mounting their horses, they rode to the cabin. After putting saddles, blankets, and tack away inside the barn, they brushed the horses.

"Luke will be taking care of you while we're gone," she crooned to the horses making sure they had water, hay, and feed for the day.

"Do you believe the horses understand you?" Killian tilted his head down at her.

"Of course. Don't you?"

"Can't say. I never talked to a horse and expected understanding like you do with the horses and Adventure."

"Maybe it's a shifter thing. But aren't angels all-powerful?

"Not as much as you'd think. It depends on the situation and the intervention required." He shrugged a shoulder nonchalantly.

"Our trip to Scotland was supposed to give us a chance to learn more about each other." She raised her arms and let them fall to her sides. "That was blown out of the water. This trip has taught me just how much I don't know about you. And me, well, my bad attributes have been on display more than my good. Pretending to be someone I'm not proved to be harder than I thought."

"You're doing fine. It's not like you are someone entirely different." His dimples winked as he smiled, and his bright blue eyes twinkled with mischief. "All will be revealed. As they say, what doesn't kill us makes us stronger." He chuckled. "Ready to travel by magic?"

"Do I have a choice?" She scrunched up her face closed her eyes, preparing for the worst. "No Scottish mists here."

"Nope, and don't have time to travel by 1878 means. Healing Waters is 325 miles northwest of here. Hold tight to my arm. I'll pick up Adventure and the bags." He sliced his hand through the air, a shimmering portal emerged, and he touched her arm.

She opened one eye, nodded, and grabbed his arm for all she was worth. The room spun. A tunnel of vibrant spinning colors engulfed them. Warm and cold at the same time, she gaped at the colors. *I can't breathe. Oh wait, I'm holding my breath.* She released the breath she wasn't aware she'd been holding. *This isn't so bad.* The spinning colors slowed and suddenly—

Chapter Fourteen

Healing Waters and the Shaman's Secrets

Killian landed feet first in the rocky soil of Healing Waters just a few feet from the canyon edge at the rushing waters of the Big Horn River. Adventure whined at his side. The bags were precariously balanced next to the edge. But no Chinoah. He jumped up and shaded his eyes as he searched for her. His pulse quickened. *Had she landed in the river?*

A few seconds later, she hit the ground a few feet from him.

Relief flooded through him. He rushed to snatch her up off the ground. "I told you to hang on. Getting separated is not something we want to happen. You could be lost in..." Her huge dark chocolate brown eyes were the size of saucers staring up at him. Her mouth opened and closed without a sound. He grabbed her shoulders and gave a little shake. "Chinoah? You all right?"

Finally, she huffed out a breath. "What the hell happened? One minute I've got a firm hold on your arm, the next a huge jolt. I saw the ground, then you slipped from my grasp, and the swirling vortex of colors sucked me back inside. Almost like some kind of warning. Weird. A second later, it spit me out."

Heart pounding like a trip hammer, he tried to

present calm for both their sakes. "Can't say. I've never had that kind of experience. But, to be fair, never ported with so many things and people before. Up until a few months ago, I was a loner. Then poof—" he made a starburst motion with his hand "—you crashed into my life. Things have never been the same. Wyoming seems to be the catalyst of all the changes in my world."

"A lucky man...er...angel you are." Chinoah brushed the red dirt off her jeans and shirt, then bent down to comfort Adventure, clearly disconcerted at recent events.

"You're fine, m'lady. A new adventure awaits around every corner—it seems."

The dog rubbed against her before turning amber eyes on him.

"He's fine too. Would you look at this place? It's beautiful."

The yellow and white marbled canyon sides appeared like wax had melted on the jagged edges before falling to the Big Horn River below. The hills or mountains seemed to be red. Large rock mounds stood ten-twenty feet high with a rust, yellow, and white marbled effect flowing over the formations.

"This has to be Thermopolis in our time. Right?" She brushed the red dirt from her jeans and fisted her hand on her hips. "Shame growing up I never had a chance to visit here. Nor what we now call Legend Rock. You can bet this time I'm going. Match the old ones' stories to what I see here." She shook her head.

"It appears so. In 1878 the land still belonged to the Shoshone and Arapaho tribes. Originally part of the Wind River Indian Reservation, it was sold to the United States in 1896, making the healing waters of Big Horn

River Hot Springs available to everyone.

"Bet the spirits weren't pleased about that," she observed, brushing the dirt from her hands. "The whole story back then—now—conflicts with what some say."

"No, the spirits aren't." Raymond's soothing voice came from somewhere behind her.

Killian whirled around and saw Raymond standing next to a petite woman with long straight black hair reaching nearly to her waist, dark eyes, and bronze skin that matched Chinoah's. He extended his hand in greeting to the shaman. "Didn't hear you walk up behind us." He turned to the woman. "You must be Lily."

The woman nodded and glanced at her husband.

"I hope this isn't an imposition. Events last Friday night led us to believe the individual we seek may be on the move and visited Wylder."

Raymond's eyebrows rose, but he only nodded. "How was your trip?"

"Uneventful," Killian said before Chinoah opened her mouth.

She found her words. "Won't you show us around Healing Waters? I'm intrigued by the rock formations and the canyon walls near Big Horn River Hot Springs. Right?"

Lily looked pleased. "Know a little about our area?"

"Not like I remember it, but it's familiar." Chinoah clasped Lily's hand. "Mr. Swiftwater invited us to visit when he was in Wylder with information."

"He told me. Welcome." Lily released Chinoah's hand.

Raymond waved his hand in dismissal. "Call me Ray."

"Speaking of information. As I was saying last

Friday in Wylder…" The scathing look Chinoah sent him had him backtracking. "We can talk business later. Tell us about Healing Waters. Belong to your tribe?"

"Yes. Still sore from your recent vocation? Without waiting for an answer, the shaman continued. "We'll visit the Healing Waters a little later today. First, Lily has a late lunch prepared for us at the house. Hungry?"

Killian's stomach growled loudly. "We are. So nice of you to invite us."

"Of course. Our pleasure." Ray took his wife's hand and walked down a path toward the huge monolith rising out of the earth. Several yards behind and to the left of it stood a small cabin with several garden plots located around the well-kept log building.

Killian started to follow Ray, but Chinoah grabbed his arm and pulled him back toward her.

"It's rude to dive right into business when you arrive at a Native American's home. It is our way, small talk first, then let our host bring up the subject of business. He knows why we are here." She hissed, then tugged him along to catch up with the Swiftwaters.

"Still, time is of the essence," he insisted. "He didn't do this song and dance last time we met."

"Ray was on our turf. The white man is known for his rudeness even in 1878." She snickered. "I'll bet he knows we're anxious to find out what he knows. He offered his help, let him get to it in his own time. It's not like this will be a slam dunk. Right?"

"No. It could get quite nasty if the demon discovers our intentions before we are ready."

"Great." The hair on the back of her neck prickled. But when she paused and turned a three-hundred and sixty-degree circle surveying the area, there was no one in sight.

"Something wrong?" Lily gently touched Chinoah's arm. The woman's soft brown eyes held her gaze.

"No. An overactive imagination." She motioned Adventure to follow. "Shall I leave our dog outside?"

Lily raised an eyebrow questioningly as she unlocked the cabin. "She's welcome inside. Not a good idea to leave a dog unattended. Need water?" Her husband held the door open for their guests. Warmth radiated out of the home, mingled with the delicious aromas of freshly baked bread, coffee, and something cinnamony.

"Yes, please." She shivered.

"You all right?" Killian leaned over, wrapping an arm around her, and whispered in her ear. "What's going on? Saw you do a three-sixty a while ago."

"Something's off. I still feel like we're being watched. But clearly, there is no one there."

Ray glanced from one to the other. "Something wrong?"

He shook his head and inhaled deeply as his stomach rumbled loudly again. "Guess I should have eaten more breakfast." He chuckled, wishing he didn't have to tiptoe around the man he was almost positive was a time traveler as well.

Ray nodded and motioned for them to take a seat around the square wooden table. "Traveling always makes me hungry too."

Lily brought over four steaming meat pies while Ray sliced up the fresh bread and passed slices over on small plates. The butter dish rested in the center of the table.

Chinoah leaned over the pie and inhaled. "This

smells wonderful." She took the plate with the bread on it from Ray. "Thank you again for lunch."

"Had a feeling you would be here today, so Lily waited on lunch to see if I was right." He chuckled. "She likes to remind me the times my intuition missed the mark."

"Not true." Lily bristled. "Only trying to keep your ego in check."

After the meal, Chinoah helped Lily with the dishes. Ray and Killian walked into the living room. Ray stirred the embers in the fireplace before tossing a couple of logs on the fire. "Do you believe your demon has discovered your intent?"

"Not my demon, but if he or she had, I don't believe we'd be standing here. A magical creature was definitely at the Harvest Ball Friday night. Detected his magic signature as if it was leaking from a badly cast spell. Or he was too drunk to control it. Couldn't get a read on whether it was an act or real."

"When the creature in question made appearances around here, he didn't disguise his magic signature. Probably felt he didn't need to, so that would lead me to believe he suspects a magic wielder is living in Wylder and could be a danger to him and his mission. You are very good at hiding your angel signature. However, your woman reeks of magic, just not a determinable type. Which could be what brought him to Wylder."

The shaman studied Chinoah as she and Lily walked into the room. "Powerful, yet, something different about you. Shifter. Correct?"

She slid a sideways glance at Killian before answering. At his barely perceptible nod, she said, "Correct."

The shaman waved his hand dismissively. "No matter. The individual you seek has been asking questions about the boundaries of the Rez. Requested a map last week. Didn't get it. Figure he'll be back sooner than later."

"Wylder is a hub for the railroad. He's been seen around the station. But as far as I know, hasn't asked about anything."

The fur on Adventure's back stood up as the dog let out a low menacing growl and pawed at the door. Chinoah got to her feet and started for the door.

"Hold on a minute." Killian beat her to the door and stepped in front of her. "Ray, Lily, is there anyone that would be watching you or us?"

The shaman shrugged. "Depends. The spirits are unhappy with the newcomer. Been quite restless when he's around. Our normally quiet river has experienced water spouts, swirling rapids, and churning water. One of our tribe members was sucked underwater.

"Luckily, several people were in the river at the time and pulled him to safety. Since then, no one from the tribe has gone near the river. Believing it was a warning from the spirits. Though our people can't do a thing about this demon interloper of yours."

"Not mine. I'm tasked to bring him back to his own time. And you? What do you think?"

"I performed a ritual at the water's edge to appease the spirits. Still, they are restless. I've had visions, one of you standing on the edge of the canyon. So I knew you were coming. The rest are muddled. A few settlers have ventured into the waters without harm."

"These are the waters you wanted me to relax in?"

The dog whined and woofed, pawing at the door

again.

Chinoah bent down and clipped the leash on Adventure's harness. "If we don't let her out, we're going to have puddles—or worse. Whatever was out there is gone now."

Ray opened the door. "Lily and I go to the pool downstream of the river. That is where we're going. Do you have swimsuits?"

He rolled his shoulders. "Yes, inside our bags. Chinoah insisted we bring them."

"You two all right going to the waters? Or would you rather stay here? The spirits have no problem with you."

"Let's check it out." Chinoah followed the men outside. "I don't sense anything now. You, girl, stand guard." She glanced down at the dog. "Seems it's all clear—for now." She gathered their swimsuits along with large towels from their bags and followed Lily and Ray. "Is there a private place to change?"

"Yes, the rocks form a three-sided area most everyone uses to change unless they are going in with their clothes on or…"

"Can't imagine doing that." Chinoah wrapped her arms around herself. "Especially with the wind."

After a relaxing soak in the calm, healing waters, Killian rolled and stretched his shoulders. Then clenched and unclenched his hands, working his arms. *Sure feels better now. Had no idea blacksmithing was so hard on the body.* Eventually, they returned to Ray and Lily's home.

"The person you are looking for is rumored to return within the next few days. He picks up supplies, enjoys the healing powers of the waters late at night, then disappears. His appearances are sporadic. Last time he was here, he was not alone. He wanted specialty items we don't have here, a map of the area, including the rez."

"Now why would he…" Killian paused, figuring a link to the land deal may be as they suspected. "We need to stall him next time he's here."

"You're free to stay with us for a few days to see if he shows," Ray offered. "I'd like to show you a cliff in the central part of the county. You'll see spectacular petroglyphs. My father claimed they were depictions of visions, spirit powers, and vision quests with people, animals, birds, fire scenes from long ago."

"I have a business to run back in Wylder. Can't be gone too long."

Ray lifted an eyebrow. "From what you've told me, you can't afford to miss him either."

"Luke expects us to be gone for a few days. If the demon hasn't shown up by that time, I can take Adventure back to Wylder, and you can stay here." Chinoah chewed on her bottom lip. Time travel had never been in her wheelhouse, but her ancestors claimed the talent through their wolves or other shifter creatures. Now faced with reality, those tales took on new meaning.

"Good plan." Killian glanced at Chinoah and Adventure.

"Unless our individual never left Wylder." She pursed her lips. "In that case, someone should be there to keep an eye on him. Though I can't imagine what he'd want in Wylder."

Ray nodded. "Tomorrow, we'll go to Legend Rock."

"Wait. Those pictures carved into the rocks are at least 10,000 years old. Right? Our storytellers claim at least three different Native American groups are responsible for those petroglyphs. Even the drawings contain possible star charts or constellations." She clapped her hands together. "I can't wait to see them." She paused for a few beats. "Would it be all right if I sketched the drawings? For research and comparison with the stories. Don't want to upset the spirits any more than they already are."

"If they object, there will be no doubt. Spirits there have been responsible for many of my visions. As to the stars, I'll leave that up to your interpretation." Ray winked at her.

Chinoah's eyelids began to droop. She stifled a yawn.

Ray grinned. "Your room is down the hall to the right."

"Thanks, but I'd like some fresh air. A nice walk would do me good before bed." She turned her warm dark brown eyes on Killian.

"Like most places out west, it's not a safe place for visitors at night, so be careful. Don't stray far from the house." Ray tossed another log on the fire. "Pretty secluded up the side of the mountain behind the house."

Killian sent her a warning glance as she bolted for the door. Once outside, she glanced around. He nodded. She shimmered, her body appearing to absorb her clothing, then shifted into the sleek black wolf and took off up the side of the mountain followed by her dog. Unfurling his wings, he stretched them out, the tips brushing the ground while the tops towered above his head.

Two powerful beats, and he was airborne, hovering slightly above and behind her, scouting for danger. For a moment, he considered sweeping her up in his arms in her wolf form. There would be hell to pay, but—Better sense prevailed, and he continued on the path she'd chosen.

Reaching the top of the mountain, she panted and flopped down in a secluded crag in the terrain. He landed gracefully beside her and stroked her soft fur. Their eyes met. She returned to human form, wrapped her arms around his neck, and pressed her lips to his in a scorching kiss.

"Thank you. I needed that," she murmured against his mouth. She trailed kisses along his jaw and down his neck. "I've been thinking. Maybe it's time we talk about our future. If we can survive this, we can survive anything."

"Couldn't agree more." He drew her against him. Her curves pressed against him heated and stirred his blood like no other. "Once this assignment is done…"

She put a finger against his lips. "Did you hear that?" She shivered. "I can't make out what is being said, but there are words on the wind."

He listened intently for several minutes. "I don't hear a thing. It's probably the wind whistling in the crevices of the canyon."

****

The scent of freshly brewed coffee wafted into the room. Killian blinked, rubbed his eyes, and yawned wide. The darkness was broken only by a ribbon of gold spreading across the horizon. They'd come in late last night.

Chinoah rolled over to gaze into his eyes sleepily. "Good morning, handsome."

"Good morning, darl'n. Slept like a rock last night

you did." Her head was in the crook of his shoulder. He gently tugged her against him and brushed his lips over hers.

She snuggled into him. "I did. I needed to run. But those sounds haunted my dreams. The spirits are trying to tell me something. I can feel it but don't understand the ancient language."

"Maybe Ray and Lily can help." His stomach grumbled as the aroma of breakfast assaulted his senses.

"Me too. I'm starved." She bounced out of bed and scurried over to the washbasin. "More modern conveniences at our cabin." Dressed in a charcoal skirt and matching sweater with turquoise stripes, she opened the door and inhaled deeply. "Yum."

"We're lucky a rich man had our cabin built with all the luxuries his money could buy until he lost it all. His bad fortune is our good luck." He rummaged around in his duffel. Deciding on jeans and a black sweatshirt, he hurried down the hall behind her.

"The food smells heavenly." Chinoah stood at the stove.

Ray turned from the sink. "I believe your man would be a better judge of heavenly."

Taken aback, Chinoah stared at Killian, who was just entering the kitchen. He appeared to ignore the remark. A slight grin played around the corners of her mouth. "Can I help with anything?"

Lily smiled at her. "No. Have a seat. Breakfast is ready."

After they were all seated around the scarred wooden table, Chinoah scooped eggs onto her plate and forked a couple of pieces of bacon. "The weirdest things happened to us on our walk last night."

Ray's expression changed from mild curiously to concern. "Was there a problem?"

"Oh no. Well, yes, kind of. I heard voices on the wind as I ran last night. The spirits, I think. Couldn't understand what they were saying. They spoke in the old language I've heard some of the elders speak."

"Interesting. Did you see anything out of the ordinary? Did the spirits appear to you?"

"No on both counts. It was more like a feeling they were trying to convey. Like I was supposed to be or go somewhere." She shrugged. "Strangest thing."

Ray forked up egg and popped it in his mouth, chewing thoughtfully. "Ever had visions? Lifelike dreams? Maybe the trip to Legend Rock will shed some light on the situation."

"I never experienced spirit visions. However, my grandmother and her mother were known as seers in the tribe." She paused for several beats. "They both passed before I was born." She turned back to her plate and scooped up the last bit of egg with a corner of her toast.

Quickly, the group finished breakfast. Chinoah helped Lily with the dishes while the men stepped outside.

"Ready?" Killian reached for Chinoah as she exited the house.

"Thought we should leave Adventure here." Chinoah grinned at Lily. "If it's all right with you."

"Fine. She's a good dog." Lily glanced at Ray.

"I'll handle the travel arrangements." Killian motioned everyone into a tight circle. Wings unfurled, he raised his arm, a shimmering portal appeared, they all stepped into the swirling gateway and disappeared.

Chapter Fifteen

Unexpected Events—A Warning or a Path Forward?

The group reappeared on the flat ground covered with bushes, that gave way to craggy rock formations rising at least a thousand feet above the earth. Chinoah sucked in a breath and took hold of Killian's hand. She leaned over and whispered. "Still feel strange." With one hand behind her back, the other tightly grasped in his hand, they followed Ray and Lily up the well-used path to the rock face.

Squinting at the sun, Chinoah searched the nearly vertical rock cliffs. At a point in the rock where two crevasses came together and formed a V, a pair of owls had built a nest. The family of owls watched them with interest. Scrambling up the rocky path to the rock panels, Chinoah stared at the crude drawings of what resembled horses, cattle, single individuals and family units, beetles, and other insects. With her fingertips, she reached out and touched a carving of what appeared as constellations.

Suddenly, the wind whistled in her ears, and her vision narrowed. She felt like a vacuum sucked her into the rock. *That wasn't possible. Was it?* In front of her and across the room, a shadowy figure bent over a table. Several other individuals stood around the same wooden

166

table. Outside a window, uniformed men on horses rode by in no hurry. A cold shiver raced up her spine as she glanced around and discovered a person whose appearance wavered in and out standing next to her. His hand outstretched, and his head shaking so vehemently that the image blurred.

*A spirit?* She assumed it was a spirit, pointed to the shadowy figure at the table. She turned toward the person intending to ask a question, but no sound came out. The ghostly figure waved his hand and disappeared. The scene before her faded away.

Reeling, she found herself on the path next to the rock, fingers still outstretched to the drawings. Yanking her hand back, she wobbled. Killian caught her before she hit the ground. The faces of Lily, Ray, and Killian swirled in front of her with the rock cliffs at their backs.

An eagle soared overhead, screaming its displeasure at the intruders. *What a strange collage. What does it mean?* The first thing she heard was the eagle's scream, then saw Killian's face contorted with worry and heard the concern in his voice.

"Chinoah. Chinoah, what's happening? Snap out of it." He hoisted her up against him and waved a hand in front of her face, then gave her shoulders a gentle shake.

The world snapped into place, and she blinked at Ray, Lily, and Killian standing around her. "I just had the strangest, almost out of body, experience." She gingerly touched the rock face. "I was sucked into that rock." She continued to describe the scene that played out in front of her.

Ray studied her. "Are the location or individuals familiar to you?"

"No. Couldn't make out any faces. By the way, they

were dressed—it appeared there were soldiers, well-dressed civilians, and Native Americans. But it's only a guess." She shook her head to try to make her thoughts more cohesive. "Still didn't make any sense."

Lily put her hand on Chinoah's arm. "Maybe we'd better start back down."

"No. No. I want to see the rest of the petroglyphs." Taking a few steps back from the rock, she took a pencil and sketch pad from her bag. Killian's steadying hands still loosely at her waist. "No more touching." Carefully she drew the figures carved into the cliffs.

Lily and Ray exchanged looks but said nothing.

"You think I'm crazy," Chinoah stated.

"No, I believe you had a vision and went on a quest that you don't understand—yet," Ray said calmly. Lily nodded solemnly.

"What do you mean? I didn't go anywhere." Her hand was drawn from the pad to the rock, but she yanked it back.

"No, but your journey's far from over." A faraway look came into Ray's eyes. As quickly as it happened, focus returned and his gaze sharpened.

She abruptly changed the subject. "You know, the demon wouldn't just walk into a trap, especially since he's become so efficient in time travel. Is there something he wants in Wylder or was it just us?" The three scenarios they'd discussed earlier didn't make sense to her. It seemed a lot of trouble for what appeared like little gain. Unless the demon had more than one agenda. Thoughts swirled in her head, making her dizzy. She shook her head in hopes of clearing it.

"I was thinking the same thing. We'll stay another day and visit the mouth of the Wind River Canyon."

Killian glanced at Ray.

"Good idea. There are different petroglyphs on the canyon walls not far from here. I'd like to see if your wife has any other visions. Clearly, I believe the spirits are trying to convey something to her. She needs to be receptive. First vision is always a shock."

"Sure was." She wasn't sure more visions were what she wanted or signed up for. Wasn't she backup for the assignment? Yet, it seemed more and more she was front and center.

After a good night's sleep, she was refreshed and almost ready to face the day. *Would there be more visions? Clarifications of the spiritual quest? God, she wished Mystic were here.*

A soft knock sounded on their door. "Breakfast is ready," said Lily. "Ray is anxious to get to the canyon. Earlier is better." Soft footfalls indicated Lily's return to the kitchen.

She and Killian scrambled out of bed and dressed. In the kitchen, Ray was already seated, and Lily served bacon and eggs. A plate of sweet rolls set in the center of the table. "We'll take whatever is left with us," she announced, putting the skillet into the sink, and slid into the seat beside her husband. The meal was quick, and they were on their way, bumping over the rutted road in the buckboard wagon. The horses seemed to know their way and slowed before Ray gave them the command.

Clambering out of the wagon, the knot in Chinoah's belly tightened. She followed Ray and Lily up the narrow footpath. Killian brought up the rear. The rock walls were multi-colored layers of red, orange, and yellow rock in a deeply eroded river canyon. A filmy form of a Native American dressed in what she considered chieftain ceremonial clothes wavered over the water, then at the canyon's edge against the rock walls. She waved her hand toward the form. "You seeing this?"

"What?" Ray looked in her direction. "Not seeing anything." He paused at a stone section where bird images and bird/human hybrids were carved into the rock. He nodded to her. She reached out hesitantly and held her hand a few inches off the face of the rock. Nothing. She blew out a breath and relaxed a little. Ray moved on.

It wasn't until the path ended and they had to pick their way down a steep slope that the Native American spirit made another appearance. Halfway down the path, her feet slipping and sliding over loose rocks and gravel, the toe of her boot caught on an arched root sticking out of the ground. She pitched forward. Her hands came up in front of her in an attempt to avoid face-planting on the rock's surface. Something cool grabbed her arms and set her on her feet. Looking into the misty, high cheek-boned face of the chieftain, she gawked. When she peered into his eyes, she felt sorrow, disillusion, and pain. She gulped in air.

*They must be stopped. You're destined to make it happen.* A male voice echoed through her mind. A picture of a log room formed in her mind then was gone. Before she could respond, the apparition disappeared, and so did the cold that had engulfed her.

"Wow. What just happened?" Killian was by her side, an arm around her waist. "How did you do that? One moment you're headed for a face plant, then next, you're upright standing on your feet." He slowly shook his head.

Ray only smiled. "The spirits appear to like you."

She related the experience. "I've had enough. Can we go back to your house?" She sent a pleading glance to Lily.

"Of course."

It was late evening when they returned to the shaman's home. Adventure greeted them at the door, then whined to go outside. After the pup did her business, Chinoah washed her hands and helped Lily prepare a quick supper. After cleaning up the kitchen, Killian again created a portal for their departure to Wylder.

"Thank you for everything, I think." She laughed, hugging Lily and Ray.

Killian clasped Ray's hand and touched Lily on the arm. "Thanks for your hospitality. We'll try to let you know what happens. Or I'm sure the spirits will." Arm tightly wrapped around Chinoah and the pup, Killian stepped into the portal and disappeared.

Chapter Sixteen

A Shocked Apprentice, A Matter of Trust, and Secrets Revealed in Wylder

Chinoah woke up disoriented and reached for Killian. His side of the bed was cool and empty. He had only black and turquoise boxer briefs or sweat pants for sleep. She had PJ's. She liked his warmth in the bed even though there'd been no further intimate contact. The events of the previous night came flooding back.

With no indication if or when the demon would return, it was necessary Killian and she return to Wylder. Ray and Lily would keep an eye out in Healing Waters.

They ported along with the pup to Wylder in the dead of night in case Luke had taken up residence in the cabin. Which they discovered he had. Even though she and Killian had discussed at great length what to tell Luke when he discovered them in the cabin, they decided to play it by ear in the morning. Only seventy-two hours had passed since they'd left. Travel from Healing Waters to Wylder would have taken at least a week or more.

Freshly brewed coffee and the aroma of biscuits wafted into the bedroom and made her mouth water. She reached beside the bed for Adventure only to discover the dog wasn't there and the bedroom door was open a crack. Male voices rose from the kitchen. She sat up and swung her feet to the floor. After a shower, she dressed in black jeans and a multi-colored pastel cable knit sweater, pulled on socks and boots. *Dog must have gone with Killian.* She wandered into the kitchen. Adventure was curled up on her blanket in the corner of the kitchen. Luke stood at the stove with his back to her. Killian was seated at the table.

"When did you...how did you... you just left a couple of days ago? Where's Chinoah?" He stammered, picked up the spoon, and continued stirring the pot. "I see the dog is back."

"Yes, she prefers to stay with us." Killian nodded to her as she entered the kitchen.

Grinning, she padded over to the chair and rested a hand on the table. "I hope Jilly knows what a catch you are." Luke yelped and whirled around. His hazel eyes huge, the wooden spoon clattered to the floor as he stood starring at her.

"A little jumpy this morning?"

A sly grin curved Killian's lips. Shook his head and grinned at his woman. "Now that wasn't nice."

She shot her angel a devilish grin then, glanced apologetically at Luke.

The apprentice narrowed his eyes at her. "Heck, learning you're working for two time travelers, chasing an unknown bad guy—demon—across the centuries, you'd be a little jumpy too."

She peered at Killian. "You swore him to secrecy and didn't disclose the entire nature of our abilities or assignment?"

"Sort of. He's still processing. Have a seat. Oatmeal and biscuits are nearly ready. Besides, this could take a while and goes down better on a full stomach, as you well know."

Gently caressing Killian's shoulders with her fingertips, she leaned over and kissed him on the cheek, then trailed kisses to his lips before taking her seat next to him. "Missed your warmth next to me this morning." She sent him a smoldering look.

"Would you like me to leave the room?" Luke said petulantly, setting the large bowl of oatmeal in the center of the table.

"Nope, we have more to discuss." Killian scooped several large spoonfuls in his bowl, then began to do the same to hers.

"Whoa. Stop—only three of those huge spoonfuls for me. Leave the rest for Luke. After all, he was kind enough to make it for us as you bombarded him with things no one should have to know."

She walked to the icebox and took out the orange juice. "Want some?"

"Sure. It's hard to come by this time of year. So I didn't use any." Luke took the biscuits out of the oven and set them on the table next to the oatmeal. "As I was telling Killian, it's a nice place you have here." He wiped his hands on the towel tucked at his waist. Scraped the rest of the oatmeal into his bowl and plopped into a chair.

"It was all set up when we arrived." She poured each a small glass of juice and sat down at the table. Biting into a biscuit, she waved it around. "Things are not always as they seem." With a nod from Killian, she continued. "No easy way to say it— Killian is a warrior angel, and I'm a Native American wolf shapeshifter." She let those thoughts settle.

Head bent over his plate, he shoveled in a spoon of oatmeal and washed it down with coffee. Luke stared up at her, choked, sputtered, and spit coffee all over the table. "Sure you are."

She yanked her plate out of the line of fire and snickered. "I assure you we're not crazy and can prove these statements." Her lips twitched as she glanced at Killian before returning her attention to Luke. "This is a serious conversation, and you are sworn to secrecy. Remember?"

He nodded but his brows drew together as he pursed his lips.

"How else would you explain us being here?"

"Never left?"

She angled her head up at him. "Why would we do that?"

"I don't know. Time travelers are bad enough, but hell, an angel and werewolf—those are mythical beings. Not real." Luke lifted the mug and took a long drink of coffee.

"Okay." She hesitated for a beat letting the werewolf comment slide for now. "Try this. How did we arrive in the middle of a blizzard with no apparent means of transportation? Thank you for saving our lives, by the way."

"How?" He eyed her suspiciously while wiping up the table, then continued to eat his coffee-laced eggs.

Suddenly the air crackled with electricity, the hair on the back of her neck and arms stood on end. Luke stared at her as the hair on his arms did the same.

"Storm is coming, and it's going to be a bad one." Luke shoved up from the table and walked to the window. The sky was blue and not a cloud to be seen.

A pop split the quiet, and Caden appeared. Luke stumbled backward. "Holy shit." He clutched at his chest, then quickly moved to a fighting stance shoving in front of her. "Who the hell are you, and where'd you come from?"

"Settle down, boy." Caden held his hand palm up in front of him. "Not going to hurt anyone." He flicked a glance at Killian and her. "Need a little help convincing him?"

Indignant, she waved her hand dismissively. "No. We got this. 'Till you barged in. Killian and I were bringing Luke into the loop, since we ported here in the early morning hours."

"Doubt Killian would approve of you stripping naked and shifting in front of this man." Caden slid a smirk in his friend's direction.

Luke's face flushed beet red as he tried circling Caden.

"Hold it right there." Caden motioned to Luke. "You're out of your league, kid."

Killian, leaning his chair back on two legs had watched the events with amusement up until now. He leaned forward. His chair returned to all fours with a bang as he stood. "No one is stripping naked in front of anyone. What brings you here, Caden?"

She fisted her hands on her hips. "How long have you been here?"

"A few minutes. Ported outside your cabin so as not to shock anyone and assess the situation. But it was apparent a little shock was required. Mystic had a really bad feeling last night. It got worse this morning. Couldn't stand by and do nothing. No idea where Becket is. He never reported back to us. Haven't talked to Nat."

"Becket and Killian kinda got off on the wrong foot when we arrived." She scrunched up her face. "Trust issues. Besides, I've learned a new trick for shifting.

Been working at it for a while. No nakedness required. Nor torn clothing." She tossed back her long mane of black hair as if to accentuate her point.

Killian put a hand on Luke's shoulder. "Luke, this is our good friend, Caden. He is the liaison to the Angel Legion. Caden, this is Luke, my apprentice at the blacksmith shop." He continued to bring Caden up to speed regarding recent events in Healing Waters and progress on the assignment.

Caden lifted an eyebrow in question. "Neat trick if you can pull it off. Mystic would be quite interested." At her eat-shit-and-die look, he paused, shifting gears. "Yeah, I've heard Becket can be difficult to get along with." He switched his attention to Luke. "So any questions, kid?"

"You're all time travelers?" Luke peered at each person in turn.

They nodded in unison.

"So everything is all right?" Caden glanced around.

"Mystic didn't accompany you?" Chinoah glanced up at him.

"Mystic is at the castle taking care of the livestock and duties left to us by you two." He smirked. "I'm making sure you two are safe. Guess I can head back to Scotland and tell my wife she was wrong."

A bit deflated and wishing they were back in Scotland instead of the wilds of Wyoming chasing something that could kill them both, she puffed out her cheeks and blew out a breath. "We just returned from Healing Waters. It is Thermopolis in present day. A shaman from there visited here a while back with info on the individual we seek.

"That person may have shown up here a couple of

days ago. Nearly spoiled the Harvest Ball. Wylder is a wild west town. Rowdy cowboys come through here all the time raising hell. Even shooting the place up on occasion. So it's hard to tell. Especially if the being can take on any form it desires."

"You have everything under control then?" Caden's brow furrowed.

"Not sure. The shaman and his wife are keeping an eye out for the demon. They are time travelers too. However, anything is possible given the circumstances we have to work with." Killian waffled a hand back and forth.

She groaned. "I miss my cell phone."

"What about him?" Caden jerked his head in Luke's direction.

"Like I said, he's my apprentice at the blacksmith shop. Lot of work for one man. Especially when you aren't used to swinging a hammer several hours a day. Luke worked for Joe, who owned the Blacksmith prior to our arrival, and came already trained. Saved our lives when we arrived in the worse blizzard seen in these parts in a long time."

"Hey, I'm standing right here," Luke growled. "I've got to get to work."

"Not a word to anyone." Killian cautioned, wagging his finger back and forth. "We'll be along shortly."

Shifting from foot to foot, Luke rubbed the back of his neck, then peered up at her. "I didn't have a chance to make the deposit yesterday or the day before. There's a lot of cash in the safe. It's been busy."

"Don't worry about it. I'll go with her to the bank." Killian made shooing motions with his hand. "Go on and open the shop."

"Yes, sir." He picked up his cowboy hat, slapped it against his pant leg, and adjusted it on his head, pulling the brim down a bit.

"Sounds good. Not that I'm buying all this, but if someone dangerous is lurking, best to play it safe." Luke ambled toward the door. "I'll saddle the horses before I leave."

"Couldn't agree more." Killian slapped Luke on the back. "You'll see we're the good guys. We'll talk later. There are a few more items we need to discuss."

Luke raised his eyebrows. "Probably best. I've enough to consider right now."

"Thanks, Luke. We'll be right behind you." Killian glanced a Caden. "You're going to need a coat, hat, and gloves. I've got extras. I'll get them." He eyed Caden. "You can ride a horse?"

"Of course. Been a while, a long while, but don't worry about me. I'll wait until you've…"

He snorted. "You'll do no such thing. You'll ride in with us as a friend. We can't afford to blow our cover now." Striding to the bedroom, he grabbed the extra outerwear, then returned to the living room and tossed the clothing to Caden.

Luke's lips twitched, but he said nothing as he exited the cabin.

"Let's go. Bodyguards." She giggled.

Killian eyed his friend suspiciously and shrugged into his coat. "What are you not telling me? Spill it."

He scrubbed a hand over his face. "It's a gut feeling. Mind if I stick around for a while since Becket is MIA?"

"Be our guest. I can use some help at the shop." Killian chuckled. "Up for a little manual labor?"

"Horses are in…" She stopped mid-sentence as

179

Luke rode up with Buttercup and Onyx in tow. "Thank you, Luke."

"No problem, boss lady." He tipped his hat to her and grinned as Killian handed him the horses' reins. "See you at the shop." He clicked his tongue and urged his horse down the road.

She glanced from Killian to Caden as she mounted Buttercup. "Someone's going to be walking."

"Nope. You're riding with me." Killian stood beside her, playfully knocking her foot out of the stirrup.

"Oh no, you don't. If you're riding with me, you'll ride behind me. Or you and Caden can ride Onyx."

"Fine." He slipped his foot in the stirrup. Slung his leg over the back of the horse and settled in behind her. Adventure yipped and ran circles around the riders.

"Been a while." She snickered as Onyx shied to the left when Caden tried to swing into the saddle. Leaning over, she caressed the animal's neck. "It's all right, boy. He's a friend. I've a treat for you when we get to the shop."

The horse moved to the other side once more, then allowed Caden to get into the saddle. Pawing the ground impatiently, the horse snorted.

"Should have introduced yourself before trying to mount him," she said with a wave of her hand and nudged Buttercup into a trot.

When they arrived at Dugan's, a line wound around the counter and toward the door. Killian quickly dismounted, tied the horses to the hitching post, stopped to motion Caden to follow, and hurried into the shop. She took an apple and carrot out of her coat pockets, offered them to the horses, then strolled into the shop with the dog at her heels. "Need help?"

"No. We got it. Just pickups…mostly." Luke glanced up only a moment as Killian slid behind the counter.

Several of the men in line shot curious glances in Caden's direction. Killian made the proper introductions quickly as he worked. Weaving in and out of the customers, she made her way to her office. After the main room cleared out, she returned to the counter. "I've a few errands to run. Killian, are you going with me? Or shall I take Caden so we don't have any trouble? Mind if I leave Adventure here while I'm gone?"

"Nope. Good idea taking Caden with you," Killian grunted.

Caden held the door for her. She glanced up and down the street before getting on her horse. The saddle creaked as she shifted and peered behind her. *Was that the man from the Harvest Ball that ducked around the corner of the building?* Not waiting for Caden, she urged her horse forward. She circled the building housing Dugan's, the Livery, its corral, and stalls but saw no one except a woman walking on the other side of the street. *Huh, must have been my imagination.*

Caden caught up with her. "What was that all about?"

"Nothing. Too little sleep coupled with an overactive imagination." She stretched and realized she was exhausted.

He raised a brow but followed her to the bank on Wylder Street. They dismounted and walked inside the bank. As usual, she greeted the teller, made the deposit, and waved to Frederick Mountroy as he crossed the lobby on her way out.

Sticking her foot in the stirrup, she paused before

slinging her leg across the horse. "Gonna stop and see Cissy before going back. After the morning Luke has had, he'd appreciate baked goods from Cissy's place." She guided the horse left onto Wylder Street. At the Wylder Side Bakery, she tied Buttercup to the hitching post and sprinted into the bakery. "Hey, Cissy." Waving, she inhaled deeply. "I'll take one of everything."

"Sure about that?" Cissy laughed and pointed out the window. "Back so soon? Whose that man waiting for you on Killian's horse?"

"Caden Silverwind, a friend of ours. Killian and Luke are busy at the forge. I'll take several cupcakes, pastries, bread, peanut butter, and chocolate chip cookies. Luke's had a rough morning." She grinned. "And I want to spoil Killian. Caden—well—he's just at the right place at the right time."

"Weren't you going with Killian?" Cissy asked, putting the baked goods in a box, and tying a string around it.

She hesitated for a beat, forgetting they were supposed to be gone. "Yeah, but it turned out to be a short trip."

Cissy raised a brow and handed the box to Chinoah. "Don't eat them all, or you'll be sick."

"They're for the men." At Cissy's look of disbelief, Chinoah giggled then added, "Well, maybe the cookies are for me."

"That's better. If you need anything else, just holler."

"Will do." She took her box and exited the bakery. Handing the package to Caden, she mounted her horse and glanced at him. "I'm going back to Dugan's. If you want to port to Healing Waters and check it out for yourself, do it from the cabin. Don't want prying eyes to see something they shouldn't."

"I'll check with Killian first. I'm more interested in what happened to Becket."

She shrugged. "Hey, any chance you and Mystic could join us here for Christmas? Now that you know where we are?"

Caden rubbed his chin. "Now that's a right fine idea. I'll discuss it with Nat when I get back. You two will have this assignment wrapped up by then?" He followed her to the door.

"Hope so. She encountered the last customer leaving. Before going into her office, she tapped Killian on the shoulder and kissed him hard on the lips. "I'll be in the office. Caden's got the box of goodies."

"What was that for?" He caught her around the waist and returned the kiss affectionately.

"Cause I can." She smirked, wiggled out of his grasp, flounced over to the counter, opened the box, and took out four cookies, then sauntered into her office, paused, and blew him a saucy kiss. After closing the door, she settled into her seat behind the desk, tallied up the day's receipts, and filled out the deposit for tomorrow. The rest of the day passed without incident.

A little before closing time, she slipped out of the office and saw Luke cleaning up his bench. Killian and Caden remained hunched over a project in the forge. She smiled at Luke, grabbed her coat, tugged on her hat, and wound the scarf around her neck. "You two about ready to leave?"

"Give me a couple of minutes, and we'll leave together." Killian took off his leather apron and slapped Caden on the shoulder. "Ready to leave?"

"More than ready. Glad you got this assignment rather than me. Tough life." Caden brushed the soot off his jeans.

Luke shrugged into his coat, hat, and gloves. "I'm heading out. See you all in the morning."

"Bye Luke. Going to Jilly's?" Killian asked.

"Yep, it's game night." Luke tugged open the door and a cold breeze swept through the building. With a wave, he quickly closed the door. Killian and Caden donned their winter gear and left with Adventure and her.

When they rode up to the cabin, the door stood wide open. She jumped off Buttercup and raced to the door, flying over the steps on the porch, the dog on her heels.

"Wait," Killian called after her, dismounting right behind her. "Don't go in there alone." He bolted in front of her, barred her way into the cabin, and grabbed the dog. "Let me go first."

"Why? You won't know what, if anything, is missing," She shoved at him, barely keeping her wolf contained.

"You can go in after I check the place out."

"You're not going in alone." Caden rushed over.

"What if it's a..." She paused, wondering if she should put a name to it. "A paranormal creature."

"You're serious?" A hearty laugh rose from his throat. "What am I? Chopped liver? Believe me. I've got this." Killian released Adventure to Chinoah and advanced to the door.

A snarl escaped her lips, but she let him and Caden enter first. Adventure escaped her hold, growling and barking, then thundered through the door between Killian's legs. Standing at the entryway, she took the leash out of her pocket, commanded the dog to her, and clipped on the leash.

After clearing the cabin, Killian lit a couple of lamps, and their home had been ransacked. It also reeked of magic mixed with another signature she couldn't identify. *Mortal mix?* Logs for the storage cubby were tossed around. The kitchen cupboards were open. The pretty flowered dishes smashed on the floor. In the bedroom, their clothes were yanked from the closet and strewn around the room. *Thank God I stowed my duffel with 1878 contraband under the floorboard in the guest bedroom.* She sprinted to the other room. The floorboards were still intact though the little desk lay on its side. All the drawers lay on the floor with contents strewn all over the room.

"Could be drunk cowboys having a good time at our expense. Maybe those you had arrested." She glanced hopefully at Killian. "Maybe they were released?"

He glanced at her and took her arm. "We all know better than that." He scratched his head. "But why? There's nothing here of value to a magical creature. Unless you brought more contraband than you told me about?" He narrowed his eyes at her.

She held her hands up in a gesture of surrender. "I did no such thing."

"Boy Howdy, what happened here?" Luke's voice came from the doorway. "Those damn drunk cowboys came back looking for revenge. Their boss made their bail."

They whirled around to see Luke standing in the doorway. "What are you doing here?" Killian and Chinoah chimed together.

"Need my stuff. I left it here this morning. Want me to get the sheriff?"

Killian shook his head. "Naw, we'll get it cleaned up and see if anything is missing first."

She blew out a breath, her heart pounding and pulse racing. "You go on over to Jilly's. Don't want you to be late." Leaning against Killian, she glanced up at him. "I didn't even hear him ride up." She peered around. "What a mess."

Chapter Seventeen

Tracking is Hard When You Don' know What Time
Or Way They Went

After trying to put things in order again, Chinoah
remained in the cabin to prepare dinner while Killian and
Caden led the horses to the barn.

"Best to take a look around in the event the cowboys
were the magic wielders. Probably want to report it. If
not—what's the downside of reporting it? Not like they
would figure a paranormal creature had been prowling
around." Killian yanked on the barn door handle, then
led Onyx inside.

Caden followed with Buttercup. "Anything of value
in here?"

"New tack, the rebuilt carriage I restored for
Chinoah, feed, hay, all costly in this time." Killian
stopped inside the barn, struck a match, and lit the lantern
next to the door. Moving the horses to their stalls and
bolting the gate, he and Caden walked the length of the
barn and checked the empty stalls and loft. Nothing
seemed to be missing or even out of place.

When they returned to the cabin, the enticing aroma
of beef stew and freshly baked bread hit them square in
the face. Killian inhaled deeply. "Smells fantastic." He
strode to Chinoah and pulled her tight against him.
Nuzzling her neck, he trailed kisses along her jaw.

Capturing her lips, he murmured, "Been quite a day." After a couple of beats as if remembering someone else was in the room, he turned his attention to Caden. "Go ahead and get cleaned up for dinner. The bathroom is down the hall to your left."

Caden gave a sloppy salute and ambled down the hall.

Chinoah rested her head against Killian's chest for a few beats, then straightened. "What if this was a diversion? Could we be dealing with more than one creature?"

"Good possibility. After your visions and talking with Ray, seems his visions and the spirits are pointing to someone messing with the negotiations in 1868. Maybe setting the boundaries for the Shoshone Reservation. Name wasn't changed to the Wind River Reservation until the 1930's. Same person or persons is using influence to arrange to turn over ownership of the Healing Waters to the settlers for less money than originally agreed upon. What we need is a current map of the reservation."

"I might have a map." She rushed into what had initially been her room, grabbed a pry bar from under the bed, and levered up three floor boards. Her bag was safe and sound, hidden away from prying eyes. Sighing, she knelt and yanked out the bag. Carefully, she tossed out silk panties and bras, three negligees, a few other items that weren't supposed to be in 1878, then triumphantly held up a current map of Wyoming. "Thought this might come in handy."

Eyes wide, Killian stared at her. "We were under strict orders what to bring on this assignment. None of those items were to come with you to 1878." He licked his lips. He felt his blood rise along with other body parts as he imagined her in only those panties, bra or negligee, legs wrapped around… He shook his head to clear the sexual haze and noticed Caden grinning.

"Looks like she had plans to seduce you in the wild, wild west of Wylder." His friend snickered.

She shrugged one shoulder. "Nat isn't my commander. Felt these items might come in handy." She carefully arranged the lingerie back into the bag, tossed the map to Killian, then replaced the bag and the floorboards. "You spoiled my surprise if there is one—now."

"Oh, no doubt you'll eventually model those for me." Smiling seductively, Killian helped her up off the floor and pulled her tight against him. "Just a matter of time."

Caden cleared his throat. "I'm still here. Would you two like to be alone?"

"Soon," Killian growled against her neck as his pulse raced and desire surged.

"She has a good point. If I were in the creature's place, I'd want to divide the troops so the designated individual could get his mission accomplished." Caden took the map from Killian and spread it on the table.

His head cleared. Killian released Chinoah and studied the map. In the northwest corner of the rez were rich mineral deposits and oil fields. "If I remember correctly, 1872 saw the government reduce the size of the reservation by approximately 600,000 acres of land around South Pass to cut out the gold fields. The Native Americans wised up and put up a decades-long fight to get the funds from the oil-rich reservation land.

"If I were a betting man, I'd say the demon and his

cohorts are looking to have the reservation land boundaries redrawn to exclude the oil land. Greed and power the demons' modus operandi. Good job Chinoah." His stomach growled as the aroma of the food aroused his hunger.

"How do we stop them? On the one hand, we have Healing Waters. On the other hand, the oil-rich land." Chinoah pretended to weigh each in separate hands.

"We can't rewrite history as the demon, and his cohorts are trying to do. The Healing Waters was lost to the Native Americans by their own agreement in 1896. The best thing we can do is follow their trail to 1868 and intercept them before they use magic to influence the boundaries of the agreement."

"Sounds like a big job for just the two of you." Caden ran his fingers through his hair. "Becket doesn't seem to be of much help. The assignment needs to be changed."

"Don't you have the right to do so being the liaison to the Legion?" He glanced at his friend. "Nat being in the present isn't available for consultation."

"We'll put a plan together, and if Becket doesn't show up. We'll run with it, let the commander sort it out. Then find out what Becket is up to since he obviously doesn't have your back." Caden grinned. "Another case of easier to ask forgiveness than it is to get permission."

"You two are trouble no matter how you look at it," Chinoah huffed. "Like your commander stated numerous times since I've known you." She snickered.

"But you love me anyway." Killian reached an arm around her and squeezed.

"True." The word was out of her mouth before she could stop it.

He pumped a fist in the air. "I knew it."

"Now, wait a minute. I was caught up in the moment." She twisted out of his grasp.

*She's said it. I knew it. Now to act on it.* He paused to relish the moment, then put his head back in the assignment.

He jumped when a knock sounded on the door. Luke stood at the door with Sheriff Hanson right behind him. Killian folded the map and stuffed it in his shirt.

Luke shifted from foot to foot beside the sheriff. "Figured you'd be cleaning this up most of the night, so I went for the Sheriff. Wylder is the wild west, but it's our home. Who's going to draw the line of acceptable behavior if we don't take a stand?"

"He's got a point," Killian agreed.

"Got a problem here?" The sheriff eyed them.

"Yes. I returned home to find this mess. We've cleaned most of it up, but still…" Chinoah took the sheriff's arm and led him through the cabin pointing out what happened. "Think the cowboys we tangled with are looking for revenge?"

"Nice place you got here. But you—" Sheriff Hanson pointed a finger at her "—shouldn't be alone out here. What if the men had still been here? Not safe." The sheriff shook his head and narrowed his eyes at Killian.

She fisted her hands on her hips and pursed her lips. "I wasn't alone. Killian and Caden were here."

"And who are you?" The sheriff looked pointedly at Caden.

"Friend of the family. Caught the train and thought I'd surprise them." Caden smiled wide.

"Instead, he got the surprise." Killian chuckled.

"I see. Without proof, hard to point fingers." He

took off his hat, scratched his head, and replaced the cap. "Anything missing?"

"Don't know. Haven't had a chance to do inventory," she retorted. "Too busy cleaning up."

In an attempt to defuse the situation, Killian said. "Have you seen all you need?"

"Guess so. I'll be in touch." The sheriff ambled across the room, took one more glance, and opened the door. "Now, don't be leaving her out here by herself. Don't want to be called out here for a murder or worse. Night."

Chinoah stomped around the room and fumed. "He didn't listen to a word we said. I can take care of myself."

"Not out here. The sheriff has a point," the men all chorused.

"We need to let Ray know what we suspect." Killian rubbed the back of his neck. "But I really can't leave again." He held up a hand before Chinoah went off. "You can take care of yourself in the present. But in 1878, going wolf isn't an option. It's a man's world out here. Women...I don't want anything to happen to you. Understand?"

"But..."

"Your little show a while back taking that cowboy down, didn't do you any favors." Luke glanced at her. "Don't mean no disrespect, but that sort of thing doesn't happen around here. Often."

"Maybe it should. I should start a self-defense class for the women around here." She paused, a steely glint to her gaze.

"Not a bad idea," Caden mused.

"When Wyoming was still a territory, legislators passed the Wyoming Suffrage Act of 1869. This act gave women in the territory the right to vote. So I'd say she'd be in good company teaching the women out in the wild west to be able to defend themselves."

"Don't encourage her. We're here to complete a mission and return to our own time. Not stir up a hornets' nest in 1878." Killian took the map out and spread it out on the table again.

"Too late. I'll talk with Cissy about putting something together."

Killian rolled his eyes heavenward. "Of course you will." He glared at Caden.

"Several of the women know how to shoot. A point you should consider. If you don't need me anymore tonight, I'm going on over to Jilly's. She's probably good and mad at me for being so late." He shuffled toward the door.

"Sorry about this," Chinoah said. "You can bring her to Dugan's tomorrow. We'll explain everything."

"That's all right. She'll be okay once I explain. Night." He closed the door behind him.

"Last thing he needs is his gal mixed up in our magic mess, and he knows it." Bending over the map, Killian glanced at Caden. "Any ideas?"

"Form a plan, check with Ray and the spirits, then go from there." Caden shrugged.

"I gotta say, I've a bad feeling about Becket since the get go. I know he's an angel sent by Nat. But... Something is just not right." Chinoah shook her head slowly.

He studied Chinoah for several seconds. "How about we table this discussion for tonight. The beef stew and bread smell wonderful. We can have a nice glass of wine and unwind in front of the fireplace?"

"I'm all for that." Caden glanced around. "Mind if I crash here tonight?"

"Of course not, as long as you make yourself scarce after we eat." Killian chuckled.

"No problem." Caden walked to the stove, lifted the lid on a pot, and inhaled. "Yum."

Chinoah padded in behind him, slapped his hand, and replaced the lid. "Things get cold fast out here and take forever to warm up." She took the bread she purchased at Cissy's out of the oven and sliced it.

Killian ambled in, took three bowls out of the cupboard, filled them with stew, and set them on the counter. "Things are slower here. No microwave." He clapped Caden on the back.

Slowly Caden passed his hand over the bowls. Steam began to rise from the bowls. At the stern eye his friend turned on him, Caden shrugged. "Not for my benefit. I'm saving you two from starvation. My story and I'm sticking to it." He picked up his bowl by the edges and dashed into the living room.

"Can't argue with that." Chinoah grabbed a potholder before getting her bowl and carrying it into the living room. She set it on the coffee table, shooed Adventure away, and returned to the kitchen for the bread.

Killian picked a bottle of wine, three glasses and followed the others. After he poured the wine, he snapped his fingers, and his bowl of stew materialized on the table next to the sofa without a drop spilled. "Shall we eat?"

"Thought you'd never ask," she said around a mouth full of stew, swallowed, and bit into a piece of bread.

A slurping sound came from where Caden sat in the

chair facing the fire. He looked up and grinned. "Sorry. Forgot my manners."

"Mystic has trained you better than that." Chinoah teased.

"But she's not here. Is she?" Caden continued the banter but finished his stew and bread quietly. "I'm off to bed. See you two in the morning." He waggled his eyebrows and grinned. "Don't do anything I wouldn't do."

"Gee, that leaves anything and everything under the sun," Chinoah teased. "Night, Caden."

He carried his bowl into the kitchen and set it in the sink before his footstep echoed in the hall to the guest room.

She filled Killian's wine glass, then topped hers off and took a long drink. "I'll take our bowls to the kitchen and be right back." She returned, sipped more wine, then snuggled with Killian. "Happy for a little downtime." She turned her face up to study his and licked her lips slowly.

He leaned over and brushed his lips over hers. She reached up, slid her hand around his neck, and deepened the kiss. His tongue finding hers caressed, teased, and explored. A pleasant taste of wine remained on her lips. Feathering his fingers on the side of her breast, he leaned over, and she arched against him. "It's time we discuss our future."

"Not until all this is over and we both survive," she whispered against his lips. "I'll not start a new chapter of my life only to have a demon snuff it out. Not going to happen."

"I've battled demons for centuries. Nothing is going to happen to us." As confident as his words sounded, he knew down deep she had a point. There was always a risk, especially in an unfamiliar time and place. *Magic should be constant regardless of the place or time, but I don't know for sure until tested. Should've asked Ray when I had a chance.*

She shifted against him, letting her fingers caress his growing arousal through his pants. Her head was resting back against his shoulder, now allowing him full access. He began unbuttoning her shirt, licked his way to her lacy bra, and slipped the tip of his tongue inside while his other hand released the catch. He sucked, his tongue teased until she moaned quietly, moving her hand inside his waistband.

"We'd better take this in the bedroom. Our guest is just down the hall."

She smiled seductively. "Where's your sense of adventure?" Her quick fingers unzipped his pants. She slid a hand inside and wrapped her fingers around him.

A shudder of desire shot through him as he pushed against her hand. "Not where my fellow warrior can witness our intimacy should we go too far. Before you— we—are ready." He swallowed hard as she tightened her grip. "Enough." He swept her up in his arms and carried her to their bedroom, closing the door with his foot.

Chapter Eighteen

A Nightmare Signals the Beginning of the End

Chinoah drifted off to sleep. Suddenly, in a dream she witnessed the man she saw at the Harvest Ball, arguing with another man in uniform sitting across from him at a long wooden table. There were others in the room nodding or shaking their heads as they all looked at a document. Voices erupted, and fists flew between the man from the Ball and the other Native Americans. The man from the Ball grabbed the uniformed man and dragged him across the table. The man grinned with a full set of pointed teeth and tossed the other individual to the ground like a rag doll—the demon.

As the thought settled in her mind, another man entered the room and held a knife to one of the others' throat at the end of the table nearest the door. This man with the knife she recognized. It couldn't—how was that possible? Suddenly a puff of air caught the document, wafted it up off the table and in front of her.

The piece of paper was a treaty dated July 3, 1868, with no signatures. Slowly, the treaty floated to the ground and disappeared. An uproar commenced around the table. The demon disappeared. The man holding a knife ran. The others in the room gave chase.

Out of nowhere, a ghostly form appeared outside the room. The creature pointed a finger at the demon who was morphing into a woman. She shook out her long reddish mane of hair, straightened her bodice, and fluffed out her long skirt. A self-satisfied smile spread across her face before she called to the knife-wielding man. The scene shifted back to the ghostly character. He shifted his position and pointed at her before fading away.

Chinoah woke up, sweat streaming down her face. The room was dark. Only a sliver of moonlight fell across the bed. *It was so real. A dream? A vision?* She shook Killian awake. The dog woofed quietly.

"I'm awake. Quit shaking me." He sleepily blinked at her. "The sun's not even up," he growled, then searched her face. "What's wrong?"

She relayed the dream to him. "Is it because it's been on my mind? Or was it a vision?"

"I don't know. Have you ever had visions before?" Sitting up in bed, he pulled her to him, brushed wet strands of hair out of her face, kissed her forehead, cheeks, nose, and finally her lips. Through the window, an orange line spread across the horizon. "It's close to dawn. Let's get up, eat breakfast, and run this past Caden."

"Shouldn't we do something?"

"What would you suggest? Until we sort it out, we can't go off all half-cocked. Good way for this assignment to turn deadly."

"I have a date and place. We can…" She climbed out of bed. Her clothes lay in a heap on the floor. The memories of last night came flooding back. Her belly gave way to swirls of desire. She wrapped her arms around him while standing on tiptoe and kissed him with wild abandonment. Blood pounded in her brain, leaped from her heart to her nether regions, and finally made her knees tremble. She knew this was the wrong time and place to act on these feelings. But God, she wanted this man—angel.

"Whoa, woman. Either we consummate our relationship here and now. Or we get the bastard that intends to change history to his advantage, completing our assignment and freeing us to explore life together." A devilish smile spread across his face. "I know your body as well as I know my own. You've made your decision. Does your mind agree?"

A blush crept up her neck. "Last night wasn't over the line, was it?"

"Only time will tell. Does it matter?" He returned the kiss with a sigh, stepped back, pulled on pants, and gathered her into him. "How do you feel now? Dream subsiding?"

She paused a couple of beats. "At this point, probably not. No, the dream is still vivid as it was when it was happening. It seems almost as if someone or something wanted me to see that date, setting and reveal who we are after could be a woman." She remembered seeing a woman across the street when she'd given chase and come up empty. "We need to confirm the date the treaty was signed or enacted or something. Was there a meeting held?"

She dressed and followed him into the kitchen, opened the cooking stove and heating stove. Killian took the dog outside and brought in wood to start a fire in each. Filling the kettle with water, she set it on the open area of the stove, hoping it wouldn't fall in and would heat up faster. Adventure circled on her blanket and lay down.

Caden wandered in, rubbing his eyes. "You two are

up awful early—after the late night."

They reiterated Chinoah's dream.

"Sounds like a vision to me. But I've never had one, only heard first-hand descriptions about them. Dreams fade. Visions don't until you act on them. Or so I've been told. That being said, maybe we have a date to reference?"

"Maybe. Or wishful thinking." Killian moved over behind his woman, resting his hands around her waist.

*He's too close. I can't concentrate.* Playfully, Chinoah propelled her ass against him, effectively backing him away. Then she donned an apron, scrambled eggs, cooked toast, and bacon, still in a daze. Her mind kept wandering to her feelings for Killian, the dream, vision, or whatever, the whole damn thing leaving her unsettled and edgy.

Smoke rose from the sizzling bacon. She grabbed the cast iron pan with a towel and shoved it off the burner. "No range of heat on this damn thing. Either too hot or too cold. I don't know how people cook on these things."

Killian set the mugs on the table and moved out of the way.

She poured coffee. "Breakfast is on the stove. Help yourself." She took the apron off, flung it across the back of a chair, and filled her plate, then plopped into a seat. She took a sip from the mug in front of her. "Not bad."

Killian eased into the chair next to her, thoughtfully rubbing his chin.

"I know that look. Spill it." Reaching over, she stroked his cheek with the back of her fingers.

"How about we travel back to 1868 a few days before the July date? Snoop around, see if we can locate anyone familiar. Caden can be our lookout. The demon and his or her accomplice, if there is one, won't recognize Caden." He got up, filling his plate with eggs, bacon, and toast. Killian glanced at his friend, nodding toward the food.

"I've not been authorized on this assignment." Caden shook his head slowly, also filling his plate. "But, it appears that Becket, who was authorized, is MIA. Therefore, I'm in." A mischievous smile curved his lips as he sat down and dug into his food.

They bounced around ideas during breakfast. Killian forked up the last piece of egg, popped it in his mouth, and wiped his lips with a napkin. He set it down on the table as if coming to a decision. "Best get to the shop and bring Luke up to speed. Chinoah, you'll need to deposit any money that's come in, then we'll meet back at the cabin, and it's off to the past for us."

Inside the blacksmith shop, Luke was finishing up repairs on Caleb's wagon tongue when Killian, Chinoah, and Caden arrived. Caleb whirled around when the door opened."

"Just the man I came to see."

Killian took off his coat. Helped her off with her parka and hung them on the hooks near the door. "What's up?"

She waved at Caleb. "Tell Lauren I said hi." She continued into her office, leaving the door open.

"Day's receipts are still out here," Luke called, scooping the invoices into a pile.

"Be right out." She grabbed the logbook and opened it on her desk.

"You know that friend of yours, Becker, or Becket something like that." Caleb kicked at the counter with his boot.

"Becket. Yeah, what about him?" Killian paused, looking over the upcoming work orders.

"He really tied one on last night at the saloon. Crazy talk." Caleb rubbed the back of his neck.

The man had Killian's full attention. "What kind of crazy talk?"

"Oh, he was single-handedly going to see that the reservation land didn't contain any oil deposits, nothing of value. He offended several of our townspeople, indicated that those living on reservation land were stupid heathens and wouldn't know what to do with the riches anyway. His words, not mine. It's a sore spot with some people around here that the government rerouted the reservation boundaries and took the gold."

Chinoah stepped out of her office. "He's a mean, miserable drunk. Just spouting off at the mouth. He doesn't like my kind. So often, we're the subject of his tirades." She snickered. "Seems his mouth would get him in lots of trouble."

"We're sorry he made a scene last night. I'll see that it doesn't happen again. We've been trying to locate him for a while. Any idea where he went to sleep it off?" Killian set aside the orders and gave Caleb his undivided attention.

"This is where it gets bizarre. Said he was going back in time to fix this shit storm." Caleb glanced at Chinoah. "Sorry for the language. Just repeating what he said." Caleb shifted his attention back to Killian. "Mean anything to you?"

"He never makes sense when he's that drunk. Did he pass out?"

"Yeah, dropped like a rock after making rude

gestures to a couple of the saloon girls. Sheriff took him to jail to sleep it off." Caleb grinned sheepishly. "Better him than my uncle. I guess."

Killian blew out a breath. "Good place for him. I'll go to the sheriff's office today and take care of things. Sorry for his behavior. He'll not be darkening the door to the saloon again."

The door banged open, and Sheriff Hanson stormed into Dugan's. "Where in the hell is your friend?" He stared pointedly at Killian. "He was sleeping off a drunk in my jail. This morning he's gone. Poof, no sign of him." The sheriff eyed him suspiciously. "The damn cell is still locked. Damnedest thing I've ever seen."

Killian and Chinoah exchanged quick glances. "Caleb was just telling me about the events of last night. I sure am sorry about his behavior. I'll see to it such behavior doesn't happen again. As soon as I find him."

"That's why I'm here. Permission to search your cabin and barn?"

Killian spread his arms wide then dropped them to his sides. "We just came from the cabin. He wasn't there. Saddled the horses in the barn. No sign of him there either. The horses would have spooked or been restless if there'd been someone they didn't know inside. But you're free to search if you feel it's necessary."

"Naw, if you didn't see anything." The sheriff took his hat off and rubbed his head. "Sure, like to know how he got out. He's not one of those magic folks?"

Killian coughed to cover a snort. "Don't think so. What do you mean?"

Chinoah blinked and pursed her lips.

"You know card tricks, reading people's minds, making things disappear. He seemed to me like one of those slick fellows that take advantage of others. You know the kind?" He shifted from foot to foot and slapped his hat against his leg.

"Oh, you mean a magician. No, I'm sure he's not one of those. Maybe the cell door didn't shut completely last night. When he woke up this morning, pushed on it, and it opened. Seeing no one around, he left and closed it."

Sheriff plopped his hat back on his head. "Possible. I guess. If you see your friend, tell him he's a wanted man." He turned on his heel and marched out.

After the door closed, Killian scrubbed his hand over his face. "Our suspicions appear to have been confirmed. Best be on our way." He turned to Luke. "We're going to be gone for a bit. Can you take care of things here?"

"Sure. I'm nearly caught up. Course, that doesn't mean a thing. Still, I'll have time to work on that project we discussed. Believe I'll stay upstairs. Don't want to get caught up in whatever is going on. However, your cabin is sure nice. Never seen anything like it in these parts."

"Good idea," Killian said.

"Maybe we should leave Adventure with Luke." She glanced at the dog standing at the door, tail wiggling.

The dog whined and pawed at the door.

"Well, maybe not," she conceded. "Could be dangerous."

Adventure barked and pawed at the door again.

Killian glanced at her. "Are you ready to go to the bank and back to the cabin?"

She nodded. "Special project?"

"Just something we been playing around with in our spare time. Nothing special."

Caden disappeared with a pop. She, Adventure, and Killian walked out the door and mounted the horses. Little was said as they rode to the bank, made the deposit, and returned to the cabin. Caden was already waiting for them.

"Ready to do this?" Killian put Adventure between them secured her leash to Chinoah's leg. "You sure you don't want to leave Adventure here?"

The dog barked and growled, her ears flat to her head.

"Give me the picture of where we are going."

She closed her eyes and pictured the room she'd seen in the vision. *It's a start.*

"Got it." He glanced at Caden." You good?"

"Yep. I'll follow you."

Killian gripped Chinoah's hands, tight lowered his head in concentration and opened the portal with a flip of his arm.

# Chapter Nineteen

## Surprises Awaited in 1868

The room was made of logs. Chinoah and Adventure landed on the makeshift bed and bounced a couple of times. "This isn't where we are supposed to land." Killian walked to the window. Soldiers on horseback filled the street inside a compound-like structure.

Chinoah joined him at the window and put her hand on his shoulder. "This looks like Fort Bridger in the Utah Territory. Supposedly, this is where the reservation boundaries were agreed upon, and the treaty signed, if memory serves me correctly. But why are we here?"

"Better question is, when are we here?" Killian shoved his fingers through his hair. "Well, at least we are somewhat appropriately dressed." He glanced at her long skirt, button shoes, and pretty blouse with embroidered flowers at the neckline and cuffs. His jeans and plaid flannel shirt blended in nicely.

Raised voices sounded outside their door. "What do you mean he wants the reservation boundaries redrawn? We did that with the goldfields." Someone gave a wicked laugh. "It won't work again."

More footsteps sounded outside the room. "We're dealing with heathens barely able to couple together a sentence."

\*\*\*\*

Chinoah's angry red face registered shock as a spirit materialized across the room. "Do you see that?" she mouthed to Killian.

"See what?" He turned in a circle and shrugged. "Guess not."

The spirit shook his head and pointed to her, then waved his hand toward the door. "You've been guided to this place and time to stop a grave travesty from changing history forever. Act now or... One of your angel's kind is involved and must be discouraged from the path he now travels."

The spirit pointed a finger in Killian's direction. "The Angel has the gift of sight. He must use it to control the outcome tonight. Tomorrow will be too late. Go now." The ghostly figure faded away.

Caden materialized into the room. "Wow, what an experience. Any idea who that spirit was?"

"What the hell are you two talking about?" Killian walked through the area the spirit had been and shivered. "Who was here?"

"The spirit that has been guiding us since Healing Water. I guess." Chinoah chewed on her bottom lip then relayed the conversation to Killian. "We gotta move now. But where? How?"

Adventure's fur stood on end. A menacing growl rose from her throat. The dog sniffed around the door and scratched just as a woman and man began arguing in close proximately to the room.

"I know that voice." Killian snarled and started toward the door.

"Wait." Caden put his hand on his friend's shoulder. "Invisibility may be of use here. Shouldn't be too taxing on our bodies since the assignment is for the greater good."

The light dawned on Killian's face. "Got ya. Chinoah, shift and follow us. Instruct Adventure to stay in here. With luck, we'll only be gone a few minutes. Surprise is on our side. Our disguised magic signatures have served us well."

Whoever was arguing outside had lowered their voices but were still there.

"This is going to be a grab and travel back to our cabin in 1878. If there is a battle, it will have to be there. Can't afford to have innocents witness our magic. I can see our path now." Killian grabbed Chinoah around the waist and kissed her hard, then put his hand on the door. "Ready?"

"As I'll ever be." Chinoah shimmered, and a golden glow outlined a black shadow that appeared around her. A black wolf emerged. Its bright yellow eyes locked on Adventure. The pup yipped once and hid behind the bed. The large wolf appeared to nod its head. Killian opened the door.

**** 

The shadows of dusk disguised the wolf as she lunged, knocking both the shocked man and woman to the ground. An unearthly scream came from the woman. The man attempted to disappear into thin air as Killian, his invisibility winking in and out, grabbed Becket around the neck and dragged him inside the room. At that point, Killian materialized and narrowed his eyes at the angel. Before the traitor angel could retaliate, Killian had his arms and legs shackled in magic restrains. *Easiest take-down ever. Becket got a little cocky.*

Chinoah thundered around the area, drawing the

attention of the soldiers headed toward the fray. She darted in between the buildings adding to the chaos while working her way back to the room where they'd materialized.

From behind, Caden slapped a crystal collar with a thin line of red running through it onto the woman's neck, effectively paralyzing her movements and any power she could wield. He tugged her into the room and slammed the door. Caden appeared, a smirk on his face. "Never saw it coming."

Becket's face had two long scratches down across his cheek and down his cheek. Blood flowed down the angel's face and stained his formerly pristine white shirt. "You are going to pay for this. You don't understand. It's all in the plan."

"I don't think so. At least not the Tribunal or Legion's plan." Killian's forehead creased in worry. "Where's Chinoah?"

"Last I saw her, there was a band of soldiers chasing her. I heard a couple of shots." Caden shoved the demon onto the bed. She screeched and spat fire, setting the bed ablaze. Caden squelched the flames and slapped a gag on the demon. "Fire breathing creature. Been a while since I've encountered one of those."

Killian ran for the closed door as a shot reported. A mournful howl split the night air. He yanked open the door. Adventure raced out, heading to the group of soldiers standing around the black wolf lying on its side a few yards from the building. The dog started barking, growling, and lunging as Killian sprinted to the wolf.

With the dog attracting most of the attention, he scooped up the wolf and ran for the room. Adventure gave one last lunge sinking her teeth into a man, then turned and rushed through the entrance to the room. Caden slammed the door.

"Get us back to the cabin. Now." Killian grabbed the dog's harness. Caden wrapped a glittering silver rope around them all and waved an arm. The portal split the air in a swirling chasm, and the parties stepped inside.

****

The cabin was dark and quiet when they arrived. Caden secured the prisoners in the spare room. Killian carried the wolf into their bedroom. Chinoah's breathing was labored but constant. Lighting the bedside lamp, he examined the bloody matted fur to discover a through and through wound had shattered the wolf's shoulder. She whined as he shifted her on the bed, cleaning the wound. When he started to bandage it, he paused and raised his hand in the air. "Bollocks to this." A bright light shone in the room. "Now I can see what I'm doing." He finished wrapping the bandage and bellowed, "Caden."

"Right here," Caden answered from the doorway. "She going to make it?"

"Hell if I'd know. Shoulder is shattered. She's lost a lot of blood. Do wolves heal differently? The bleeding had stopped by the time I brought her in here."

"You healed her once. You'll have to use angel magic to do it again," Caden said in a matter-of-fact tone. "Conflict or not."

Killian brought his charcoal-gray wings from his back, the black tips brushing the ground as he picked up Chinoah, wrapped his wings around her, and eased down on the bed. A warm golden glow surrounded them both. "You'll need to get our prisoners to Nat. Or at least notify him."

"Already thought of that. Communication in these time travel assignments is a bitch," Caden commented. "I've reached Mystic telepathically. I'll tell you it was difficult over the years. But never the less I got it done. Hopefully, she will arrive soon with Nat. He and I can transport the prisoners for trial at the tribunal. Mystic will stay here with you and Chinoah."

"What about my cousin's place?" Killian muttered, stretching out on the bed.

"That's the least of our worries right now. But, if I know our commander, he'll leave a warrior angel there to watch the place until Tavish and Jaden return."

"They'll never trust me to take care of the place again," he growled. *I really look forward to the respite each year. Now, my retreat is no longer a secret. Should have been Chinoah's and mine this year.*

"Tavish knows what you are and your duties. He'll understand. Now rest. You look a little worse for wear yourself. Healing is going to take a lot out of you."

"Gee, ya think," Killian snarled.

Caden merely shrugged. A loud pop came in the other room. Adventure jumped up from the side of the bed and ran barking out of the room. "Believe reinforcements have arrived. It's just like you to leave me to explain everything to our legion commander. He's going to be pissed."

"He should vet his warrior angels better. Becket is scum." Killian's eyes closed. "Talk with you later."

****

"Well, well, if sleeping beauty hasn't come around." Nat stood over the bed, glowering at him.

Killian blinked at the bright sunlight filtering through the curtains in the bedroom. "How long have I been out?" He glanced down to see that Chinoah had reverted to human form in his arms. *Gotta be a good sign.* He carefully rolled her under the covers as he drew his wings from around her and into his back. Getting to his feet, he peered at his scowling commander.

"A day and a half. Luke stopped by to check on things. The young man indicated the special project was finished. Caden filled him in on the situation here. Guess he's aware of who and what you are?"

"Work too closely with him to avoid it." Killian jerked his chin toward the door. "Can we take this discussion into the other room?"

Mystic silently padded into the room with the pup on her heels. "I'll take over from here. She'll be fine." She shook her finger at Killian, then poked him in the chest with a brightly painted orange fingernail. "This is absolutely the last time I trust you with my best friend."

A sharp come back was on his lips, but he thought better of it in front of his commander. "We'll discuss this later."

"Have it your way." Mystic flounced across the floor to stand beside Chinoah's bedside.

He and Nat moved into the living area where a cheerful fire snapped and popped in the hearth. Caden relaxed in a chair across from the fire. One booted foot resting on his knee, a smug expression on his face. "Her bark is worse than her bite." A snicker escaped his lips.

Killian filled his commander in on the events that led to traveling back to 1868 and the fort. "Don't believe the assignment was compromised. It was pure chaos when we took the demon and Becket down. Chinoah was in wolf form when shot. Her dog, Adventure, ran interference. Then we returned here."

Nat nodded. "Good job. I've ordered another squad of warrior angels to transport the prisoners to avoid any claims of impropriety Becket may try to lodge. I had no idea he'd gone to the dark side."

Chapter Twenty

Healing Process and a Decision for Eternity

Chinoah blinked her eyes open and stared at Mystic. "Is that really you? What are you doing here?"

"Apparently, you can't stay out of trouble. I leave you alone with Killian, and what happens? You get yourself shot and shatter your shoulder. That injury is going to be sore for a while. But... it's healing nicely."

She licked her lips and sighed. "Adventure?"

"She's fine. Curled up on the blanket near the fire after being chased out of this room. Played the heroine, so I heard. Saved your butt with Killian's help. Don't you want to know if Killian is all right?" Mystic chided with a grin.

"Of course, he's all right. He's an angel, isn't he? Adventure is a sweet dog. We're taking her back with us." She shifted in the bed and attempted to sit up. "Ouch." She grabbed at her shoulder.

"So I heard. You're here for a while. No more time travel until your shoulder is healed." Mystic helped her friend sit up, put her dressing gown on, and tucked pillows at her back.

"Great. Oh wait a minute, we can celebrate Christmas with my friends in town. There's a Christmas Ball at the hotel. Lauren made a beautiful emerald green gown that sparkles for me, just for the ball. Then there is a Festival on Christmas Eve at the schoolhouse. The students are going to put on a Christmas show and snacks provided afterward. Everyone will be there. Violet has worked extremely hard on the program."

"Sounds like you've embraced this town." Mystic glanced around the cabin. "Not as rough as the rest of the town appears." She grimaced, clicked her tongue, and shook her head. "About that gown, it'll match your bruising by that time. Not to mention navigating the ice and snow in a long gown with your arm in a sling protecting your shoulder."

She knew her friend was right but chose to ignore it for now. "No this cabin is nice. We were lucky the rich man that had the house built, went bust in the goldfields, and had to sell it. Still, cooking is a nightmare." She shook her head. "But Cissy's baked goods are to die for."

"Did I hear my name?" Cissy bustled into the bedroom with a basket of baked goods on her arm. "What happened to you this time? Several women of the town are ready to take self-defense classes from you. We can hold them in the bakery's backroom or…" She put the basket down on the bed. "Guess it'll be a while." Glancing in Mystic's direction, Cissy held out her hand. "Don't believe we've met."

"Cissy, this is Mystic, Caden's wife. She came from Scotland to spend Christmas with us. I was just telling her about the Christmas Festivities in Wylder."

"Happy to meet you." Cissy smiled as she took out loaves of bread, cinnamon rolls, and a chocolate cake. "Figured you wouldn't be baking for a while. Put a stew in your icebox."

"Oh, thank you." She leaned up to hug the woman.

"Buck and I have to get going. Just wanted to make

sure you two were all right. Luke said there was a skirmish out here with some out of towners. Indicated Killian and Caden took care of the situation, but you got caught in the crossfire."

"Yeah, you know me, wrong place at the wrong time." She tried to shrug her shoulders but winced. "I don't think the cowboys will be back here again."

"Did you tell the sheriff?" Cissy wanted to know.

"No. He didn't do a thing last time but tell me not to stay out here alone. This time we just handled it ourselves. Nothing he can do now that they're gone anyway."

" True. But…" Cissy hugged her lightly. "See you later. Have to plan for the ball. You're still going?"

"That may be up in the air." She jerked her chin to her shoulder, repeating what Mystic had said.

"You will at least make it to the Christmas Eve Festival at the school. Violet and the kids have worked really hard on it."

"I'll do my best." She smiled.

"Do about what?" Killian sauntered into the bedroom and grinned. "What are you women plotting? He leaned over and brushed a kiss over Chinoah's lips, lingering for a beat or two. "How are you feeling?"

"Sore, but I'll be able to go to work tomorrow."

He raised an eyebrow. "You sure? We can get along without you for a few days."

"It will take me longer than that to fix what you two goof up. I'll be there at least to take care of the books and make the deposit. Besides, I want Mystic to meet Laurel and pick up some things at Cissy's bakery."

"Guess I'll have to get the carriage out. Did I hear you say you're going ahead with plans for the women's self-defense class?"

"Yes, you did." Cissy fisted her hands on her hips. "We women need to be able to protect ourselves. Seems like the railroad has brought more undesirables to town than we expected."

"'Fraid Chinoah won't be much help for a while."

"Mystic can step in and help with the classes while she's here." Chinoah volunteered. "I'd like to hold a couple of classes before Christmas."

Mystic nodded. "Happy to help."

"Seems you're a little incapacitated with that shoulder." Killian frowned.

"I come from a long line of quick healers." She pushed up from the bed, winced, and eased back down. "Tomorrow, it'll be much better."

"Of course it will." Killian grabbed her slippers and helped her to her feet. "I supposed you want dinner with the rest of us."

"You betcha." She leaned against him for a beat. Then stood on tiptoes and kissed him. "Thanks for saving me," she whispered, then straightened. "Don't want you men conniving behind my back."

"Wouldn't dream of it, darl'n." Killian's Scottish burr was more pronounced as he returned the kiss.

She made it out to the living room under her own power and settled on the couch facing the fireplace. *The warmth sure feels good.* Surveying the room, she wondered what happened to Nat and the prisoners. Better they're gone or keeping out of sight. Don't need to explain the arrival of more people. She started to get up when Buck and Cissy walked to the door to leave.

"No, you stay right there," Cissy commanded, waving a hand. "We can see ourselves out."

She relaxed onto the couch. "We'll work out the logistics of the self-defense class tomorrow. I'll stop by the bakery and look at the list you have, then determine how much room we'll need. Maybe some of the older children would watch the younger ones for a couple of hours. Or we could hire an older child to watch the younger children during the class."

"We'll work something out. Just like when we started the quilting get together." Cissy plopped her hat on her head and took her gloves out of her pockets. Buck helped her with her coat.

"If you don't mind my two cents. It'd be best to hold the class during the morning, so the women could return safely to their homes in time to cook supper without having to use what they learned." A snort escaped Killian's lips as he eased down beside her.

She narrowed her eyes. "Not a laughing matter."

"He's got a good point." Cissy nodded. "We want to avoid any more trouble. The streets of Wylder sure aren't safe after dusk. Not to mention some men would have a fit if dinner wasn't on the table when they got home."

"Night." Cissy and Buck walked through the door. Caden closed it after them and leaned back against the door. "What an experience."

"Where are Nat and the prisoners?" Chinoah surveyed the room.

"The two warrior angels Nat requested to escort the prisoners appeared just as Buck and Cissy walked up the step. Nat accompanied them and the prisoners to present time to stand trial at the Angel Tribunal. Caden and I gave them our statements. So that should tie things up in a neat package."

"We'll be going home soon?" She was surprised at

the disappointment she felt saying those words.

"Whenever you want. Figured you wanted to stay for Christmas. Luke is ready to handle the blacksmith shop on his own. We'll hire and start training another apprentice before we leave, so after Christmas works perfectly."

"But you wanted to spend the holidays with your cousin in Scotland."

"Darl'n, we've plenty of time. Don't worry about it." Killian smiled down at her. "Let's warm up the stew and add Cissy's bread to it for supper."

"Sounds like a plan." Chinoah started to push up from the chair.

"Don't you dare. I got this." Mystic sprinted into the kitchen. "Killian, how do you start this thing?"

He laughed. "Be right there." Entering the kitchen, he waved a hand over the stew, making steam rise. "Tonight, this is how we do it."

"Dinner is served," Mystic called as Killian set out bowls and sliced the bread.

The couples ate quietly. Chinoah finished her stew and two pieces of bread with a wide yawn.

"On that note, Mystic and I will turn in. Sounds like we have a busy day tomorrow." Caden took Mystic's hand and led her down the hall to the guest room.

"Not very slick." Chinoah giggled.

"No, but we're alone." He wrapped his arm around her shoulders, careful not to jostle her injured one. Leaning over, he took her mouth with his. Tingles of desire shot straight to her nether region. It was time she informed him of her decision. She caressed his cheek with her hand and wrapped her good arm around his neck. Her fingers tangled in his reddish-brown hair that waved at the back of his neck as she deepened the kiss. She could feel his heat and arousal on the outside of her thigh. "We need to take this into the bedroom where I can have my way with you without fear of interruption."

His smoldering gaze swept over her. "Are you sure? This is a decision…"

"Not to be taken lightly. I know."

He stood cradling her carefully against his chest and carried her into their bedroom. With his foot, he closed the door and walked across the room to settle her on the bed. He unbuttoned her dressing gown eased it over her head. Male appreciation lit his brilliant blue eyes as his gaze slowly slid down her body, followed by the teasing touch of his fingers.

The thrill of his stare ignited a firestorm within her despite her shoulder and the arm wrapped tightly against her body. Her gaze wandered over his chest as the muscles worked under his shirt. He was a fine specimen of a male. She wanted to trail her finger down his naked flesh, feel the heat and caress his length. "Wait, this is no fair. I'm naked. You're fully dressed."

"Easily taken care of." Pausing, he kicked off his boots, tugged his partially unbuttoned shirt over his head, and removed his pants, letting them pool at his feet. Sitting on the edge of the bed, he eyed her like a lion sizing up his prey.

Her breathing increased as moisture gathered between her legs. She reached out to him, her fingers caressing the contours of his chest, washboard abs, and finally exploring his growing manhood. Smiling, she licked her lips and tore her gaze from his impressive package to look into those deep blue eyes filled with desire. "I'm ready to take an angel as my mate for eternity. Provided he's as good in bed as he is with foreplay."

He snickered, sliding along her good side on the bed. "Never had any complaints." Leaning on an elbow, he took her chin in his hand. "I love you, Chinoah." He leaned over and kissed her nose, cheeks, eyelids, then took her mouth hungrily. Relaxing his elbow freed his hands to explore the soft lines of her back, waist, and curves of hips.

She moaned softly as his fingers feathered along the inside of her thigh, then teased the curls between her legs. He caressed the little bundle of nerves at her center and slid a finger inside. Instinctively, her body arched toward him. "Enough of this teasing. I want the real thing." His eyes widened with surprise when she flipped him on his back with her good arm and straddled him. On bended knees spread wide, she hovered over him, allowing penetration in tiny increments until he grabbed her around the waist and seated himself fully inside her. "Is this enough of the real thing?"

His hips undulated slowly at first as she rode him, her head flung back, and her back arched. "Oh my God, you're good." She desperately needed more of him, and right now.

"Glad you approve," he panted, grabbing her around the waist, and increasing the rhythm. She reared up and ground down against him, crying out as waves of ecstasy throbbed through her.

He kept pace with her until the pleasure subsided. Spent, she eased her upper body on top of his, her nipples tingling against his hard, moist chest.

"You did that on purpose." She accused enjoying the feeling of him.

"You bet I did, and I'm not done with you yet." Easing out of her, he carefully returned her underneath him, crawled between her legs, and thrust into her again. She moaned and spread her legs wider as he pressed deeper and deeper with more urgency. With a deep growl, he shoved up into her, held and thrust again.

She howled, then screamed, "Killian!" Digging her fingernails into his back, she writhed under him just before she crashed over the cliff into ecstasy again.

"Well, there will be no doubt what happened tonight." He leaned on his elbows and rested his forehead against hers and smiled. "You feel so damned good." He nipped at her lips before soothing the bites with the tip of his tongue. Parting her lips with his tongue, he began a sinuous dance with hers. Eventually, he released her and brushed his lips over her moist ones murmuring. "Your shoulder okay?

"We heal quickly, but I'm going to regret this in the morning, but it was so worth it.

Thoroughly satisfied, her head fell back. Through a slit in the lacy curtains, she gazed at the sliver of silver moon floating in the star-strewn night sky. Beautiful and pure, her easy mating with only him for eternity. Somehow the act of joining her with him didn't seem as scary. After all they'd been through, it seemed—right. In the dark, she lay curled against him, drifting toward sleep, and smiled. "I guess that's it."

He stroked her back and tenderly brushed his lips over her forehead and whispered, "It's done. You're mine for eternity." He joined her as they succumbed to a peaceful sleep of the sated.

****

The aroma of freshly brewed coffee and the sun's

rays awakened her. She glanced over at the sleeping angel in her bed and smiled. Shifting in bed, she discovered that her shoulder wasn't the only thing sore this morning. Her angel was built to please. Leaning over she brushed her lips over his. "Good morning, husband."

His eyes blinked open and he smiled. "Good morning my darl'n wife."

"No. Don't mistake this for me relinquishing my right to a full on wedding in your Scottish castle when we return. You got that?"

"Of course, I assume you'll want a Native American ceremony as Mystic had?"

"Yes." She yawned and stretched her arms above her head. "Last night was unbelievable." Her fingers danced over his bare chest.

"There's more where that came from," he said seductively and winked at her.

"Hey, you two. Breakfast is ready. Better get a wiggle on." Mystic hollered from the kitchen.

"How does she know we're awake?" Chinoah whispered, scrunching up her face and relaxing across his naked body.

"Bad news. That's not all Mystic will know. Caden too. When a warrior angel takes a mate, those closest to him automatically are aware." He raised a brow and grinned at her. "Especially when that mate lets loose with a long howl during the act. Under these circumstances, time travel and all, you're lucky that Nat and the legion won't know until we return."

"I'm never leaving this room." Chinoah buried her head in his chest and pulled the sheets over her head.

"Okay by me." He reached over and caressed the curves of her body.

A loud, insistent knocking sounded on the bedroom door. "Come on. We need to get to town so I can make arrangements for a Christmas ball gown. Or at the very least, get more of the scrumptious goodies from Cissy. By the way, congratulations, you two." With one final knock, Mystic's footsteps grew quieter as she returned to the kitchen.

"Race you to the shower." Her feet barely hit the ground before Killian swept her into his arms.

He smiled down at her. "So what do I get when I win?"

"No fair you cheated."

"You didn't set out any ground rules. So…I win." He nuzzled her neck as he carried her into the bathroom, careful to step into the shower first.

Fifteen minutes later, fully dressed, they sauntered into the kitchen.

"Coffee?" Mystic held out a mug. "I don't know how you live like this. That stove is impossible. Takes forever to warm up, then burns everything. At least Caden knew to feed the wood stoves and warm this place up. Does the wind always blow around here?"

"Just like it does in present-day Wyoming." She snickered, relieved her friend didn't tease her about her new marital status. Breakfast was on the table. She was starved. After the four of them scarfed down the meal and did the dishes, the men followed by Adventure went out to hitch the horses to the carriage.

The ride into town was uneventful, to her relief. She'd had enough excitement for a lifetime. Killian stopped the carriage in front of Dugan's and helped the women out as Caden tied the horses to the hitching post.

"This is a quaint little town." Mystic turned in a slow

circle outside the blacksmith shop.

Chinoah motioned her friend into the shop with her good arm. They walked through the main room, waved to Luke then walked into her office. "Have a seat." She pointed to the chair in front of the desk. "Need to take care of the books. Then we can stroll to the bank and make the deposit. The Lowery's Dress Shoppe isn't far. After the dress shoppe, we'll stop back at Cissy's place for baked goods and dessert for dinner." She pulled out the ledger and receipts. "The people are really nice here. Well, most of them. Not what I expected when we first arrived." After she made all the entries, she glanced over at Mystic. "Wait until you meet Laurel, she is so talented, and her little boy is such a doll. She'll have a dress whipped up for you in no time."

"I'm still not sure you should be traipsing around in a fancy ball gown with that arm in a sling. Puts you off balance. Don't want you more damaged than you already are." Mystic tilted her head in her friend's direction with a crooked smile. "Maybe just the festival would be enough?"

Closing the ledger, she tucked it back in the desk. "We can still go see Laurel. Even if we don't go to the ball, the dress would be a great thing to remind you of Wylder." She lowered her voice to a conspiratorial tone. "Watch out for Mrs. Lowery. She can be a bit crotchety. Keeps a rifle under the counter. For a good reason."

She recounted the encounter with the cowboy across from the dress shoppe. She waved her hand dismissively at Mystic's look of horror. "That's what brought about talk of a woman's self-defense class." She shrugged one shoulder and changed the subject. "If we can't go to the ball, the next day we can go to the festival at the schoolhouse on Christmas Eve. It'll be lots of fun. The whole town will be there. Then we'll have to make arrangements to return to our own time," she said in a wistful tone.

"You really like it here." Mystic observed.

"You get used to it. Wouldn't want to live here. I like my creature comforts too well. But Wylder and the people do grow on you"

Chapter Twenty-One

Christmas in Wylder and Return to Scotland Where a Surprise Celebration Awaits.

The days leading to the Christmas festivities were filled with shopping, wrapping packages, and decorating. Killian and Luke interviewed young men from town for the apprentice position. Jon from a nearby cattle ranch seemed a good fit for the position. The blacksmith shop was busier than ever. The new hire worked out well and wasn't afraid of hard work. This set Killian's mind at ease, leaving Luke in a good position to succeed.

They laid the ground work for leaving, telling everyone he had to return to Scotland to take care of family business and didn't know when or if he'd return. Luke would be the only one who knew the real story.

"Not going to get much use out of the surprise for Chinoah." Luke glanced over at him.

"Yep. But I plan to take her, Mystic, Caden and myself to the Christmas Eve Festival at the school in the sleigh. Seems we've enough snow to be a good ride. After we leave, the sleigh, horses, and cabin will be yours."

"I'll never be able to pay you back." Luke said.

"No need. You keep our secret and that's all repayment we need."

"It's been a pleasure knowing you. You'll be missed around here." Luke snickered. "And Chinoah, well there'll never be anyone like her."

"I imagine that's a good thing. But at least the feathers she ruffled by teaching the women's self-defense classes got smoothed over."

"Yeah, after all was said and done, the men saw the benefit of the classes. I'm glad Jilly took them. I hope she never needs to use them, but I feel better knowing she knows the basics to protect herself. Especially since she'll take over the bookkeeping from Chinoah and could be alone in the shop at times. In fact, Jilly's father is talking about teaching her mother and Jilly to shoot."

"That's great." Killian glanced around the shop. *Not much longer, and I'll be gone. It's been one hell of a ride. A tough life, but I've made some great friends.*

Caden came around the counter and put his hand on his friend's shoulder. "Bittersweet, my friend."

The door to the shop blew open. Chinoah and Mystic rushed in with bundles and boxes. "Christmas's all done," the women chorused. Adventure jumped up from her place on the rug by the wood stove and barked her greeting.

Chinoah stopped to scratch the pup behind the ears, then ambled over to Killian and put a hand on his soot-covered arm. "It's Christmas Eve. Aren't you going to close the shop early so we can get ready for the festival? Everyone will be there. Heard the children rehearsing earlier this week. They were outstanding."

"Yep, Just finishing up Caleb Holt's wagon tongue. He'll pick it up after the festival tonight on his way home." He gave the hammer one more swing and flattened the red hot seam. That'll do it."

Luke came over to examine Killian's work. "Great job. I'll be off. Gotta pickup Jilly. See you at the festival." Luke swung into his coat, put on hat and gloves. The wind whipped through the room as he yanked the door open and waved before hurriedly shutting it behind him.

Killian picked up the blanket he had warming by the fire. "Let's go. This should chase the chill until we reach the cabin." He helped Chinoah into the carriage. Tucked one side of the blanket around her and lingered over her, gazing into her eyes. "I love you." He took her face gently between his huge hands kissed her soundly.

"Newly mated," Mystic said with mock disdain.

Caden helped Mystic into the carriage and tucked the other side of the blanket around her. "Wasn't too long ago you had those stars in your eyes." He kissed her and climbed up to sit beside Killian. The horses pawed the ground and snorted, restless to be off.

He clicked his tongue and slapped the reins, encouraging the horses to head home. A quick stop at the cabin and the couples changed into their festive best. Chinoah loaned Mystic a bright red skirt, light green blouse, and tan button-up dress shoes. Chinoah donned the emerald green skirt that shimmered when she moved, a festive red and green blouse with puff sleeves, and her favorite black button-up shoes. The men dressed in their finest Sunday trousers and shirts.

Earlier, Killian brought the blanket in and placed it over the rod in front of the warm fireplace. When he checked the quilt, Adventure rushed to the door and whined, shifting her gaze to each person. "Sure you can come. The kids at the school would miss seeing you." He opened the door, motioned to Caden to keep the women inside, and slipped outside.

When Caden could keep the women contained no more, Chinoah pulled open the door and sucked in a breath. "Oh, Killian. It's beautiful." She flung her good arm around his neck and gave him a smacking kiss.

In front of the cabin hitched to Onyx and Buttercup was a bright red sleigh. Light snow fell as she circled the sleigh, running her hands over the sleek edges, flicked the silver bells on the side, and inhaled the fresh scent of pine boughs tucked in the front curve. The horses shifted anxiously in their fancy leather harnesses with red tassels and small silver bells. Adventure circumvented all the excitement, raced to the sleigh, and jumped in.

Mystic stepped around Caden and whistled. "Wow." She paused. "Killian, did you make this?"

"I did," he said proudly. "With help from Luke. Come on. Get in before we all freeze standing out here." He climbed in after the women, spread the blankets across all of them, then slapped the reins, encouraging the horses forward. The snow crunched under the horses' hooves as the sleigh and its passengers made the short trip to the schoolhouse. Lights shone in every window of the building.

It was cozy and warm inside the building. Most of the town had turned out. Tables filled with snacks of all kinds lined the walls of the room. The children milled around singing platforms waiting for their chance to perform.

Luke waved from the back of the room with Jilly on his arm, standing next to her parents. Killian gave him the thumbs-up sign. Greetings of "Merry Christmas" echoed through the schoolhouse. Violet clapped her hands together. "Please, everyone, find a seat."

The children performed their songs, then everyone joined in to sing Christmas Carols. Afterward, Chinoah and Killian visited with several groups of people introducing Caden and Mystic. They congratulated Violet. Joined a table with Cissy and Buck, sitting across from Caleb and Laurel with her son, Jesse who sleepily rested his head on his mom's shoulder.

Killian sat and enjoyed the sights and sounds of their friends and Wylder. What had started as a terrible assignment turned out to be one he would remember forever. As everyone began to gravitate toward the door, he decided it was time. "We're going to call it a night. Merry Christmas, everyone." Killian pushed up from the table. "Caleb, I'll meet you at Dugan's."

"Yep. Then we're going home too. Jesse's had enough fun for one night." Caleb took the now sleeping boy from his wife and followed Killian's group to the door.

Arriving at the blacksmith shop, Killian unlocked the door and lit a couple of lamps while Caden stirred the embers in the woodstove and added a few logs. Luke beat Caleb to Dugan's

"Jilly and I decided to stop to see if you needed any help. Figured this would be the last chance to say goodbye and good luck."

"Thank you, Luke. It's been great working with you. I'm sure you'll do fine until we meet again."

Luke's eyebrows lifted. "You coming back?"

"Stranger things have happened. As you know, the story is that I had an emergency in Scotland that needed my attention. Didn't know how long I'd be gone, or if I would be able to return. That left me a little window of returning." He smiled and clapped Luke on the back.

"Take care. Don't let that gal get away."

"I won't." Luke paused then gave Killian a one armed hug. "Thanks so much." He turned and did the same to Chinoah. "Goodbye. This town will miss you both." He turned on his heel and walked out.

"Wow this is harder than I figured." Chinoah wiped a tear away. "I had the same problem when I told Cissy and Laurel." She paused. "And Buttercup and Onyx."

"Guess you've covered all your bases. I'll tell Caleb tonight. I imagine Cissy already shared our departure with Buck. Also let most of the town people we worked with know what was happening."

"At least we got to spend Christmas Eve with Wylder." Killian engulfed her in a hug. She sniffled and rested her head on his chest.

The door banged open and Caleb strode in. "What's this? I hear you're leaving Wylder."

"I was going to tell you tonight. Emergency in Scotland. Gotta leave tomorrow. Luke will take over Dugan's and my cabin. With your permission, I'm going to give him Buttercup and Onyx. He'll take real good care of them."

"I know it. Sorry to see you go. Aren't coming back, are you?" Caleb clasped him on the shoulder then, offered his hand.

He gripped Caleb's hand in a firm shake. "Stranger things have happened. But probably not." He shoved the wagon tongue toward Caleb on the counter. "Good as new."

The rancher examined the item. "Great work. Too bad you're leaving. Good blacksmiths are hard to find. Solid friends are even more difficult. Good luck to you and Chinoah. Taking the dog with you?"

"Sure will. Chinoah, won't part with her. Luke will do a good job for you."

Caleb nodded.

Chinoah and Laurel stood by the woodstove, heads together. They hugged, and Laurel shifted Jesse to the other hip glancing at Caleb.

Caleb gave a hearty laugh. "That's my not-so-subtle signal, it's time to go. Again good luck to you." He strode over to Laurel, took the little boy, and slipped out the door with a wave.

"I'm going to miss our friends. Tough life out here, but friends mean a lot." Chinoah wiped her cheeks with the back of her hand. "Are we leaving tonight?"

"No. Figured we'd get a good night's sleep and leave at first light." He switched his gaze to Caden and Mystic.

Caden shrugged. "Works for us."

The ride from the shop to the cabin was a quiet one. Killian pulled up to the cabin door to let the women and Adventure out.

Chinoah, remained in the carriage. "I'll go to the barn with you." She smiled and took out two apples she'd gotten at the festival. "A Christmas treat for Buttercup and Onyx." She offered them to the horses, stroking their neck, leaning her forehead against theirs. "Luke and Jilly will take good care of you."

He and Chinoah finished brushing the horses. "Ready?"

She nodded. Arms wound around each other they strolled back to the cabin. "We should pack tonight, so all I have to do is feed the pup. We can be gone at first light."

\*\*\*\*

The next morning dawned unusually sunny and bright at first light. Dressed in pink jeans and a jeweled sweater, Chinoah was in the kitchen feeding Adventure as the others trouped in. "Everyone ready?"

"Yep," Mystic and Caden chorused.

"Wow, don't you look nice." Killian grabbed her around the waist and swung her in circles. He lowered her enough to brush his lips over hers.

"Put me down." Chinoah squeaked against his lips.

"Your wish is my command." Dropping her to her feet, he picked up their bags. "Adventure's stuff in here?" He hoisted one of the bags higher than the others.

"Yep. Fed and watered the horses too. They're set for the day."

"Luke will be here before he heads into work, I'll wager." Killian chuckled. "My former apprentice likes the comforts the cabin affords. Can't blame him."

"What if he and Jilly get married?" Chinoah blurted.

"We'll have to return," Killian answered with a wink. "Made arrangements for him to get in touch with us through Ray." The Scottish angel raised an arm and created a swirling portal shimmering in blues, greens, and yellows. Chinoah, thankful for the quick healing of shifters, held tight to Adventure as the two couples stepped through. Killian's voice boomed, "Next stop, the Scottish Highlands."

The Scottish mists blanketed everything as the couples emerged slightly behind the standing stones in the shadow of the silvery full moon sinking toward the horizon. "A bit of a walk from here," Killian said.

Chinoah put the pup on the ground and glanced questioningly at her angel. "A run?"

"What a fantastic idea." Mystic chirped.

"Yeah, I could use a little wing time, myself." Killian arched his back and brought forth his wings.

"I see how this is going to go." Caden unfurled his wings. "Race you to the castle."

"Wait," Killian boomed. "We have to be in human form before we reach the castle, just in case Tavish has guests over the holidays."

"Agreed." Chinoah shimmered and shifted, followed by Mystic. They thundered across the ground with Adventure in hot pursuit.

The angels took flight, keeping up with their mates until they reached the land surrounding the castle where they all took their human form. A red and green banner decorated with pine cones and ribbons declaring "Welcome back" rippled in the breeze.

"Looks like someone is expecting us." Chinoah grinned.

The massive wooden door to the castle swung open. Tavish and his wife rushed out. "Merry Christmas."

"Merry Christmas." Killian returned the greeting. "How did you know?"

A sly grin spread across his cousin's face. "Ya don't think ya be the only one with Dugan talents?" He grabbed Killian in a bear hug. "Glad you made it back with a successful assignment under your belt. Come in, come in." Ushering the couples in, he stepped aside before the dog bowled him over as she rushed into the castle. "Who's the new member of your clan?"

"Adventure. Chinoah insisted she return with us." He shrugged.

The huge Christmas tree he and Chinoah had brought in and decorated still stood in the main room. Festive ribbons, pinecones, and decorations adorned the walls and staircase. The presents he'd left for his cousin and his wife were still under the tree, along with four more and a bone.

Killian scratched his head. "Your mum has the sight and passed it on?"

"Yep. Along with a bit of Fae magic that runs through our lineage. Thought it was about time I owned up to it. Since you dumped your angel status on us last year." Tavish winked at him and glanced at Chinoah. "I see a wedding in our very near future."

Jaden giggled. "I'm so excited for you." She hugged Chinoah. "Welcome to the family. I've been studying your people's wedding ceremonies since Tav told me."

Peering at her best friend, Chinoah smiled. "Mystic is kinda the expert in Native American wedding ceremonies. So I'd like to consult with her about the wedding. If you don't mind, I would love to hold the ceremony here at the castle."

Clapping her hands, Jaden laughed. "Aye. Aye."

"Hey, before you women run off and plan the wedding of the century, could I borrow Chinoah for just a couple of minutes?"

"Well, okay, if you promise to bring her back unharmed." Mystic teased.

"Guaranteed." Killian led her to a little room off what was originally the great hall and closed the door. "This is not how I planned this but can't slight my cousin for his exuberance either. I had no idea he had the sight and magic buried deep in our ancestry. Anyway." He pulled out a little carved wooden box and opened it. Inside was the deepest purple amethyst solitaire on a silver band. "Wanted to make it official." Slipping the ring on the all-important finger of her left hand, he brought her hand to his lips, kissed it, then whispered against her lips. "For eternity."

"I believe we already made it official." She held her hand out and watched the stone shimmer in the sun's rays shining through the window. "For eternity."

## A word about the author...

Tena Stetler is a best-selling author of paranormal romance. She has an over-active imagination, which led to writing her first vampire romance as a tween to the chagrin of her mother and delight of her friends. After many years as a paralegal, then an IT Manager, she decided to live out her dream of pursuing a publishing career.

With the Rocky Mountains outside her window, she sits at her computer surrounded by a wide array of witches, shapeshifters, demons, faeries, and gryphons, with a Navy SEAL or two mixed in telling their tales. Her books tell stories of magical kick-ass women and mystical alpha males that dare to love them. Well, okay there are a few companion animals to round out the tales.

Colorado is home; shared with her husband of many moons, a brilliant Chow Chow, a spoiled parrot and a forty-five-year-old box turtle. When she's not writing, her time is spent kayaking, camping, hiking, biking or just relaxing in the great Colorado outdoors. During the winter you can find her curled up in front of a crackling fire with a good book, a mug of hot chocolate and a big bowl of popcorn.

http://www.tenastetler.com